MAVERICK PREACHER

Clay Purnell was hopeful that his posting to Capra would be peaceable enough. However, on his very first day in town he rode into trouble, and from then on things seemed to get worse. Although loath to use his .45, Clay found he had little choice — and his likeness to a notorious bank robber didn't help either! A bitter range-feud was brewing and nightriders were on the prowl. For a reluctant gunman, Clay was destined to shoot a lot of lead.

Books by M. Duggan
in the Linford Western Library:

THE TREACHEROUS TRAIL
TROUBLE IN BIG SPUR
THE TIN STAR
THE HANGMAN'S NOOSE

M. DUGGAN

MAVERICK PREACHER

Complete and Unabridged

LINFORD
Leicester

First published in Great Britain in 1995 by
Robert Hale Limited
London

First Linford Edition
published 1997
by arrangement with
Robert Hale Limited
London

British Library CIP Data

Duggan, M.
Maverick preacher.—Large print ed.—
Linford western library
1. English fiction—20th century
2. Large type books
I. Title
823.9′14 [F]

ISBN 0–7089–5005–1

Published by
F. A. Thorpe (Publishing) Ltd.
Anstey, Leicestershire

Set by Words & Graphics Ltd.
Anstey, Leicestershire
Printed and bound in Great Britain by
T. J. Press (Padstow) Ltd., Padstow, Cornwall

This book is printed on acid-free paper

1

TO the dust-covered weary man the pool below looked inviting. It had been a long time since he'd been swimming. There were folk waiting on his arrival so it'd be best to forgo the swim but he knew he wouldn't do it. He shrugged they'd just have to wait. As was his custom he eyed the land spread out below him. Not a sign of life, no betraying dust cloud to announce that he'd soon have company. He grinned he was going to have his swim.

Hoofs on shale; the sound was slight but enough to waken the girl. She sat up, unalarmed because she knew that whoever was descending the other side of the creek could not see her, could not be aware of her presence, for the rocks around her provided excellent cover. She had chosen the

spot for this very reason. And the ancient horse which had brought her here would make no sound for she now prudently wrapped a bandanna over its nostrils. She was taking no chances for there were some murderous varmints on the trail these days. Men who'd consider a lone woman an easy target. She was pragmatic about these things. She listened. After a while, after he and his horse had drunk he'd move out.

The sound of a tuneless voice and splashing water told her she was off target. She'd not been the only one attracted by the water of Lizard Head Creek, so called because the shape of the pool had put some unknown *hombre* in mind of a lizard's head. Reaching for her Spencer Carbine rifle she cautiously peeped out. Her eyes fell upon the items of clothing spread out upon the flat white rocks which surrounded the pool. Itemizing the clothing she realized that he'd stripped off completely before submerging himself. She, for the sake of decency, had, of course, kept her undergarments on.

Red longjohns! Well, at least he could have kept them on, she thought indignantly. He turned his head slightly in her direction affording her a partial side view. She sucked in her breath in sudden shock. She'd seen that face before, on a wanted poster, nailed up on the wall of the Red Garter Saloon, her place of work, and a place she wanted to get out of. Yes, she'd remembered that face in particular simply because the reward, to her way of thinking, was stupendous. Enough to get her to some place decent, a civilized place, a place she could start over.

The man was the notorious bank robber. Chivers he was called. And he was wanted dead or alive. An excellent shot with the Spencer Carbine she was sorely tempted to kill him forthwith. It would be less trouble that way, less risk to herself. In fact she sighted the Spencer Carbine on his head. One squeeze of the trigger and the deed would be done.

"Goddamnit it. I just can't do it." She lowered the rifle. But she sure as hell wasn't going to let him ride out. She intended collecting the reward. She'd been given her chance and she intended taking it. She wouldn't take her eyes off him for one moment.

Whistling cheerfully, Clay Purnell waded out of the water. He was at peace with the world, a man who knew his place in the order of things. Life looked good. Or it had done until now. Clay froze, instinct telling him his predicament was dire.

She stepped out from the rocks catching him unaware with his pants down so to speak, and the Spencer Carbine she was toting was pointing at his midriff.

"Raise your hands, mister," she shouted.

"Yes ma'am." He obliged damn quick. From the look of her she was just as liable to accidentally squeeze the trigger as to do it deliberately. It seemed she'd also taken a dip but had modestly kept on her undergarments for she was wearing them now and nothing else. Obviously she'd been stretched out in the sun drying out.

"There's no cause for alarm, ma'am. I'm a decent man. I'm . . . "

"I know damn well who you are. You're Chivers."

"No ma'am that ain't so. The fact is I do bear a resemblance to Chivers. He's my cousin."

"You damn liar," she exclaimed. "What do you take me for? A fool?"

He took her for an attractive woman but wisely kept that thought to himself. "So what is your intention, ma'am?" he asked, hoping it was not her intention to blast him; after all Chivers was wanted dead or alive.

"My intention, you varmint, is to deliver you to town and claim my rightful reward. And don't you be forgetting they ain't particular. Dead or alive it says. It don't make no difference."

A firm believer in the hereafter he

was not afraid to meet his Maker. But not yet awhile. He wasn't ready. Not whilst he was in his prime. "I'll go with you peaceably, ma'am. There ain't no reason for you to commit murder!"

"You're a fine one to talk about murder," she snapped.

"Chivers ain't never shot anyone down in cold blood," he defended his kin. "He's a thief not a killer."

"He's a bank robber. That is you're a bank robber and I reckon they'll hang you. Don't that bother you none?"

"No, ma'am." He eyed her speculatively. His state of undress did not seem to perturb her as might be reasonably expected. "You work in the saloon don't you."

"What if I do!"

"And you're intending we both ride into Capra as we are right now. For decency's sake, ma'am, we'd best put our clothes on."

"Naturally I was getting round to that." She eyed him uncertainly. "Best get your duds on but if you make a move towards that Peacemaker I'll blast you. Too bad you're destined to hang for you ain't a bad-looking *hombre*!"

Very slowly and carefully Clay put on his clothes taking care to shake out his boots. He could have had that rifle away from her he reflected; all it would take would be a handful of dirt in the face, a desperate move but one likely to work. If he'd been Chivers he would have done it. He grinned. He was heading for Capra in any event and had no objection to riding along with her. She'd discover her error soon enough and her face would be a sight to see.

Gracie was in a dilemma. She couldn't see how she was going to be able to put on her gown and keep him covered. As the need to keep him covered was great she was forced to decide that she'd have to take him in wearing her petticoat. She whistled and her horse ambled out.

"Back away, mister, whilst I retrieve this Peacemaker."

Obligingly he did back away.

As she stooped to pick up the cumbersome .45 still trying to keep him covered with the rifle he knew he could have jumped her easily and wrestled that rifle from her hand. But there was no need for that. He was content to let her make a fool of herself, content to ride along with her. He grinned. Doubtless she hadn't realized the view she presented stooping for the gun was a mighty handsome sight.

Straightening up, catching sight of his smirking face she swore softly for she realized what the varmint had been looking at. And it also occurred to her that this was too easy. Doubt assailed her. Suppose he'd spoken the truth, suppose he was not Chivers? But the only way she could find out was to take him into town.

"Mount up," she ordered. "And don't be fool enough to make a run for it. I'm a crack shot and I won't have no difficulty in picking you out of the saddle."

"The thought never crossed my mind, ma'am," he rejoined swinging easily into the saddle. "How come you reckon yourself to be such a fine shot?"

"On account of necessity. The cooking-pot would have stayed empty many a day if it was not for the critters I brought home."

"How come you left the farm?"

"That, mister, is none of your damn business. And don't think I don't know what you're about. You aim to get my guard down so that you can jump me." Holding her breath she hauled herself into the saddle but he made no move to grab the gun. She eyed him curiously. "The prospect of dancing at the end of a rope doesn't seem to perturb you none, mister. How come?"

"Ma'am, I've already told you. I ain't Chivers. And mighty soon I aim to prove it to you. Got a handle have you, ma'am?"

"My name! It's Grace. Gracie they call me. How come you're interested?"

"If I come asking for you I'd best know your name."

Misinterpreting his words she snapped, "Mister, you won't be afforded a chance to buy what I've got to offer."

He winked. "I wasn't thinking of buying. But I reckon it's reasonable for you to make amends when you realize your mistake. Ain't you admitted it was in your mind to kill me out of hand?"

"You're some smooth talker, mister. If I've made a mistake, which I don't reckon on for a minute, I'll make amends."

She had been considering shooting him down without giving him a chance purely for her own self-protection, of course. Men of his sort, desperate men with a rope waiting for them, would not balk at shooting down a female.

"I'll hold you to it," he promised, damn glad that he'd decided to ride to Capra rather than take the stage. Hell, if he'd been on that stage he and Gracie might not have become acquainted.

They ambled along at a slow pace. She was no horse rider. Clay began to whistle. "How come you want this reward money so bad?"

"I've had a belly full of that two-bit town." In reality she wanted to start over again, open a shop maybe but he'd laugh at that.

Cresting the knoll they looked down at the sprawled buildings of the town. "I reckon some kind of celebration is going on." Clay eyed the bunting, the tables laden with lemonade, cakes, roasted meat. He knew who it was all for.

"Town's getting itself a new lawman." She paused. "And a Bible thumper. I guess it's for the minister. Not all the folk in Capra will be glad to see Sheriff Mark Gaskill. And that ain't surprising!"

"I'll ride on down with you if you insist. But if you do insist you'll be the joke of the town for months to come.

I'm expected in Capra. Do you realize how many times I could have had that Spencer Carbine away from you? And in the event that I was Chivers do you think he'd let you take him so peaceably? Now, if you'll just allow me to reach into my vest pocket there's a letter inside which will tell you who I am. I ain't lying. I ain't a liar."

"Sure as hell you ain't Sheriff Mark Gaskill. He's a damn sight older than you."

"I never said I was."

"Then who do you claim to be apart from being Chivers' cousin?"

"I'd be grateful if you didn't spread that information around." He pointed. "All that below, it's intended for me." He shrugged. "I'll give it to you straight. I'm Capra's new minister."

"But this can't be. You ain't dressed right. You're sporting a .45."

"Read the letter. Now if you ain't got no objection I reckon I'd best change into my working suit." He eyed her in some surprise for instead of the curses he had expected her face had turned scarlet.

"Don't you worry none," she declared, twisting her hands, "There ain't no way folk will learn that we've been keeping company. That I saw you at the creek. If I meet you on the sidewalk I won't embarrass you. As far as I'm concerned we ain't ever met."

"You ain't a liar are you?" he enquired, unbuttoning his shirt.

"I sure as hell ain't," she rejoined angrily.

"Then I'll expect you to keep your promise."

"What promise." An incredulous expression crossed her face. "You're joshing."

"Nope." He stepped out of his boots. "I aim to collect. But not now. At the appropriate time."

"Then in that case," she snapped, clearly flummoxed, "I'd advise you not to meddle in what don't concern you." So saying she kicked vigorously and got her ancient nag moving downwards towards Capra.

Clay waited awhile. He ought to have reminded her to put on her dress. He guessed her appearance in her undergarments would occasion no little outrage amongst the good ladies of Capra. Especially if they caught any of their men casting an appreciative eye. After a decent interval he rode down himself.

"Welcome, Minister." The mayor a short, rotund individual with a pink, shining head stepped forward, round blue eyes almost popping out of his head when they came to rest upon Clay's Peacemaker. Tied low on the hip the .45 was attracting a deal of comment. "You are the minister ain't you." The Mayor was obviously having second thoughts.

"That's me," Clay rejoined with a grin. His gaze came to rest upon the *hombre* standing alongside the mayor, dwarfing the shorter man. A man as tall and powerfully built as Clay himself.

Like Clay the man wore a .45 tied low. Clay's eyes dropped to the man's highly polished boots, and he frowned as his eyes came to rest upon the vicious gold star spurs. Expensive suit he noted, silk shirt, gold cufflinks, weather-lined face; this man was no pen pusher. Clay pegged him as a rancher, a prosperous one, a pillar of the community. Nevertheless there was something about the man which made Clay's hackles rise.

John Brewes couldn't believe the man standing before him and the mayor was the minister, Reverend Clay Purnell, a man who'd come so highly recommended, a man who worked tirelessly for the good of others; a paragon if the letters of recommendation were to be believed. Not being a fool, John Brewes had smelt a rat. Indeed it had occurred to him that the folk in Beaver Creek had wanted to get rid of their minister mighty bad.

A short, fat female pushed in front

of him. Maria Brewes beamed at the minister. What a handsome man he was. Blond, shoulder-length hair, blue eyes, such a broad chest and, most important of all, there was no Mrs Purnell. He had yet to find the right woman.

Brewes scowled at his daughter. Unfortunately she'd taken after her mother, Mrs Brewes being short and fat.

"I'm Maria Brewes. And this is my pa. Biggest and richest rancher hereabouts," she added by way of incentive.

"Ma'am." Politely Clay lifted his hat thinking that she was mighty discomforted beneath that blue silk gown; he reckoned she was laced up mighty tight. And he did not care for the way she was looking at him.

"Allow me to introduce you to folk, Minister." She took his arm. "It was provident you were not here sooner, one of those painted creatures from the saloon actually rode into town wearing only her undergarments. I hope you'll insist that the town makes it a rule that these creatures stay off the sidewalks whilst decent women are abroad."

Uttering a grunt of disgust John Brewes turned away. Squinting into the distance he watched for the stage. That was why he was here. To welcome the new lawman. He didn't give a damn about the new dog collar and if Maria thought that she'd be able to get Clay Purnell interested then she was a damn fool.

He rubbed his chin. Purnell and Gracie had ridden in from the same direction. Not that he'd dare mention that. His eyes narrowed; there was something about Clay Purnell that he didn't cotton to. And why the hell would the minister need a Peacemaker? What kind of minister arrived looking for all the world like a hired gun?

His scowl vanished. A genuine smile of welcome spread oyer his face. Gaskill was here. And about time. There'd been arguments. Mrs Gaskill having flatly refused to come to Capra. Hell, Brewes couldn't understand why Gaskill hadn't upped and left the woman. All they were was trouble and a sensible man ought to know it.

Instead of halting mid-way down Main Street the crazy fool in charge of the coach kept right on coming, a cloud of dust following in his wake. Those amongst the crowd more alert than their fellows moved themselves rapidly aside. A table laden with plates of food went flying. A woman screeched out as she slipped over and two other women fell upon her. An oath escaped from John Brewes, what the hell had gotten into Hodge?

With an ear-splitting whoop Hodge brought his team to a halt just short of the crowd. A wide grin split his toothless face. He'd learned them. And he could hardly contain himself. Could hardly wait to see John Brewes' expression when he broke the good news.

"What the hell?" Brewes snarled,

resisting an urge to yank the oldster down from his driving seat. Not lacking in common sense Brewes had to acknowledge that it was long too late to try shaking some sense into the old reprobate.

Eyeing the sweating horse-flesh Clay saw that the team had been pushed hard. And if the others failed to realize it he himself knew that the old man would not have pushed the horses without damn good reason. Pushing his way through he also noted the smell of whiskey which hung around the oldster. Half drunk and still able to stop that damn team just where he wanted to stop them Clay thought admiringly.

"We need the doc and we need him bad," the oldster hollered playing up to the crowd. He hiccuped. "Mr Brewes, sir, it's my painful duty to inform you that Capra won't be getting itself a fine upstanding lawman after all."

"You drunken bum." John Brewes jerked open the stage door. And let out a roar. "Goddamnit someone find the doc. It's Gaskill. He's been shot."

Clay stood back as they flocked around the stage. Why in tarnation should Brewes be so almighty concerned? The oldster had clambered down and now, unnoticed, was helping himself from the tables.

"Is he dead?" Clay asked.

"Maybe." The oldster took a mouthful of ham.

"Don't happen to know who shot this fine upstanding lawman do you?"

"I surely do. I reckon he deserved it an all. Last person you'd think of gunned him down. Ain't you guessed yet? It was his wife and, unless I'm mistaken, son, which I ain't, these folk have gone loco. I reckon they're planning to hang her, here and now. I ain't the only one around here had a mite too much whiskey. Leastways I know what I'm about which is more than can be said for some. That fool woman has gone and told them what she's done!"

2

THE mood of euphoria which had been present before the stage had rolled into town had vanished. The crowd was turning ugly. Brewes, Clay noted had distanced himself from the crowd. Nevertheless there was an ugly look upon Brewes' face which told Clay the rancher entirely approved of the suggestion that had been put forward.

Catching the minister's eye, Brewes grinned sardonically. He knew what was about to happen now. The darn fool was about to take on the town.

Clay moved through the crowd, using his elbows to move aside the folk in his way. Gaskill lay stretched out upon the dirt, an ugly splash of red staining his fancy satin vest. Mrs Gaskill stood beside the body, red-eyed, dishevelled.

"I say hang her. An eye for an eye

the Good Book says." The speaker was a black-bearded farmer Clay had noted earlier. He'd also noted the man's worn-looking woman sported a discoloured eye.

"It don't apply in this case," Clay drawled. "Gaskill ain't dead. He ought to be but the Lord has seen fit to spare him."

"Well he's near enough dead as makes no difference," the farmer persisted.

Clay thinned his lips. The man was obviously keen to see a woman dance at the end of a rope. It didn't happen often. Clay had heard tell that the folk hereabout had once hung themself a female widelooper. He wondered whether this farmer had had a hand in that. And whether Brewes had known about it and had done nothing as now!

"You two men!" He got their attention. "Get the sheriff over to Doc's surgery, and as for you friend," he regarded the farmer, "as I said

Gaskill ain't dead. Now just supposing you were to hang Mrs Gaskill here and Gaskill himself recovers, what do you think is liable to happen? You don't know. I'll tell you. He'll come gunning for the men who killed his wife, the ringleaders so to speak. And in case it slips your memory Gaskill favours a gut shot; he don't like to see those he guns down die too quick. Gaskill likes his work and his work is killing folk. The man has never made any secret of it. I'm puzzled as to why you folk have seen fit to import him!"

"That's really none of your concern, Minister," the mayor rejoined. "But you have a point. The sheriff ain't dead so it wouldn't be fitting to hang Mrs Gaskill." As mayor of the town he'd be the first one Gaskill would come looking for should the man recover. Every word the minister had said was true. Gaskill was a cold-blooded killer, a killer who hid behind his badge.

Clay smiled. "Good, I knew I could count on you, Mayor. Mrs Gaskill can stay with me till we know one way or the other." He hid his relief. Shooting down his new parishioners, and he might have had to blast them had they persisted, was not the way to begin his ministry. "Now, Mayor, if you'd like to show me to my place." He held out his arm, "Come along, ma'am. You ain't got nothing to worry about."

He followed the mayor wondering if the good folk of Capra knew what they'd be getting in Gaskill. Wrong-doers in Gaskill's town weren't given the chance to face a judge and jury. Gaskill was a firm believer in six-shooter justice. He thinned his lips. He had an unpleasant hunch that he'd find out soon enough just why Capra had hired itself a killer, a man who took backhanders to look the other way. A cattleman's lawman. Gaskill had no time for dirtbusters.

During his first night in Capra, Clay was forced to pass more time than he would have liked praying that Gaskill would not die. Not that he cared about

Sheriff Gaskill. He was no hypocrite and would not pretend that he did.

It was Mrs Gaskill and himself that he was worried about. If the lawman died the town might yet try to lynch the woman and in that event Clay knew he'd have to take on the town. And if he took on the town he'd have to use the Colt .45. And if he used the Colt .45, in all probability before folk saw reason lives would have been lost.

After breakfast, trying to look untroubled he headed for Doc's place.

"Bastard's going to make it," the doctor, a rotund man with a cherub face, observed. "Too bad. I practised once way back in a town which had Gaskill as its lawman. Hell, I ain't seen so many funerals since."

"You're sure," Clay persisted.

"I know my job, son," the doc replied, in a put-out voice. "The Lord ain't going to take Sheriff Gaskill yet awhile. You ain't needed here."

His first job was to return home and inform Mrs Gaskill that she had failed in her attempt to kill her husband.

"It was your prayers that saved him. God bless you." Much to his embarrassment she tried to kiss his hand.

"I reckon it was more a case of the Devil taking care of his own." Clay retreated hurriedly.

* * *

As a cowhand he'd worked damn hard; as a minister he'd always found the time passed slowly. Wearisome; he was a man of the open plains not a town dweller, bcing confined to town sometimes was pure punishment.

He resisted the temptation to sally into the Red Garter on the off-chance that Gracie might be around. He kept on towards the livery barn. He had a good horse and it was his duty to exercise the animal. If anyone chose to query the amount of time he managed to spend out of town he was quick to point that out.

"Howdy son." An oldster was seated upon an upturned pail chewing baccy vigorously. "So you're the new man the town's been expecting. You're a darn sight different than the last one.

"What happened to the last one?" Clay enquired. The oldster spat. "The fool always did tend to work himself into a state over the wrong-doings of others. Upped and died during a sermon he did. About how man should not turn upon his brothers it was." The oldster cackled. "You ain't heard yet have you, son? Ain't you wondered why the town saw fit to employ Gaskill at more than the going rate?"

"Thought did cross my mind."

"Well, if you want to know something I'm the man to ask." The oldster cocked his head and peered at Clay like an inquisitive bird.

Clay grinned broadly. He was prepared to play along. "I'd thank you kindly if you could tell me why this town is so keen to employ Sheriff Gaskill."

"Well, seeing as you've asked and

seeing it ain't exactly a secret, leastways it's a secret they all know about, there ain't no reason why I can't oblige." The oldster paused, and lowered his voice to a conspiratorial whisper. "There's woollies on the way. And when they get here . . . "

Clay thinned his lips. "All hell is going to break loose."

If there was one thing any self-respecting cattleman detested more than the dirtbusters it was sheep. And with reason, for the animals cropped the grass down to the roots.

And Brewes being the kind of man he was would detest the woollies more than most.

"*Hombre* named Simpson has bought the land adjoining Mr Brewes." The oldster cackled maliciously. "Bets are being taken on how long Simpson will last."

"Got any baccy to spare?" Clay enquired. He felt like a slug of whiskey but it wouldn't do given his calling to be seen going to one of the saloons.

"Sure thing, son." The oldster, his expression approving, cut him a plug. "Got me a stone jug inside," he volunteered. "We'll go on in if you've a mind. I appreciate you can't be seen out here wetting your whistle."

"Lead on old-timer," Clay rejoined grimly. It would be impossible for him to stand idle whilst folk murdered each other. His every inclination was to side with the cattlemen but seeing who he was he could not follow his inclination. He must remain impartial.

* * *

Dan Hater viciously reined in his horse before the livery barn.

"Positively disgraceful." The woman's voice was sharp and clear.

Hater swung down from the saddle, glowering for a moment or so. He thought the woman was referring to him. But the two matronly figures didn't even give him a glance. Both were glaring at the closed door of the livery barn.

"He's at the jug. Has to be," the speaker continued.

"But he came so highly recommended. And I heard tell that he spent the night on his knees praying for the sheriff."

The first woman sniffed.

The door of the livery barn creaked open. Two men emerged. Hater eyed them with some interest. The old wizened fellow with wisps of grey hair and a stubbled chin was obviously the ostler. The other galoot to Hater's disbelief, wore a black suit and dog collar. The smell of whiskey filled the air.

"Howdy ladies. Looking for me." Clay beamed at the two disapproving females. "Here I am and happy to oblige."

"You've been drinking, Reverend Purnell."

"Is that a fact," Clay rejoined. And so he had but he was far from drunk. And he recognized the man watching this exchange between himself and the ladies. "Hell!" Staggering towards the horse trough he plunged his head into the water. And held it under. His stomach churned. The prospect of having to use his Peacemaker loomed before him.

When Clay had passed by the Red Garter he had not gone in to look for Gracie but he had allowed himself to peer over the batwings reasoning there was no harm in so doing. Gracie hadn't been around but he'd recognized the *hombre* tapping his way towards the piano.

Childs. The all but blind piano player. He'd been at the Red Garter ten years according to the oldster and folk knew no more about him now than they did the day he'd got down from the stage. Only his name now wasn't Childs. It was Smith. Just Smith. Plain and simple. Nothing else. No other handle.

And as for Dan Hater, the polecat was a low-down bounty-hunter. Clay surfaced spluttering and shaking his head. Hell, it had to be coincidence. Hater couldn't be looking for Childs.

Clay was relieved to note that the women had bolted. Probably thinking he'd been intending to force unwelcome attention upon them. And why the hell did Hater have to wear ear-rings made out of threaded bones? And a necklace to boot. The man sure as hell liked drawing attention to himself Clay thought sourly. And Hater had all his attention but not for the reason Hater imagined.

Clay's stomach churned again. Hell and damnation he thought, if Hater were after Childs then he had no choice: he had to kill Dan Hater. Fair and square naturally. Two men facing each other on a dusty street. The fastest gun walking away, the slower man destined to be planted six feet under. That was the way of it. It was a bad way to be sure but there was no other way available. Words, pleas, why they'd just be wasted upon

Hater. The man would split his sides laughing.

Flipping the oldster a coin, the bounty-hunter grated, "Take good care of my horse, old man. Do you hear now?"

"Yes sir." The oldster, despite the whiskey, caught the coin, pocketing it with alacrity.

"Mind telling me who you're after, bounty-hunter?" Clay enquired mildly.

"Why the hell should I." Hater gave the minister his attention. He noted the heavy .45 tied low upon the thigh.

"I need to know a man's name before I can start praying for him," Clay rejoined mildly.

"What the hell," Hater shrugged dismissively. "It's Childs. The *hombre* dropped out of sight ten years back but the bounty is still good. I've checked."

"How come you run him down?"

"Just luck. A saloon girl thought she recognized him."

"She tell anyone else."

"Naw. Upped and died. Bad lungs."

Clay nodded. "It happens." He cleared his throat. "I'm a plain speaking man, Dan Hater, and I guess I've got to speak plainly now." He narrowed his eyes. "You ain't going after Childs."

"The hell you say!" Hater exclaimed in disbelief.

"The fact is," Clay continued mildy, "the fact is I owe the man. Twenty years back Childs saved three lives. My pa, folk were fixing to hang him for something he hadn't done. And I reckon me and my cousin would have been blasted trying to save him. Childs reckoned Pa was innocent so he intervened." He shrugged. "You've got a choice. Ride on out. Forget about Childs or reach for your piece. You'll have to kill me before you go after Childs."

Dan Hater, much to the surprise of the oldster, threw back his head and laughed heartily. And then the laughter faded. He nodded.

"I can see you ain't got a choice in the matter," he rejoined. "Seeing as you're beholden to Childs. But I ain't riding out. If you're set on dying then I can oblige you."

"Let's get on with it."

Hater nodded. "Sure. But it's got to be out on Main Street."

"Hell no. The less folk seeing me hauling iron the better. I've got my good name to think of."

"So have I," Hater rejoined. "I ain't having folk accusing me of gunning down a minister without giving him a chance. We're doing this fair and square. Folk have got to see us. Know that I didn't use no tricks to gun you down."

"Hell. Lead on then." Clay hesitated. "Perhaps in the circumstances we'd best walk side by side. Tell me, Hater, are you prepared for the hereafter? Now's the time to start asking forgiveness."

"You conceited jackass. You really believe you're good enough?"

"I sure do." Clay could see that the fact that he was walking down Main Street alongside Dan Hater was occasioning a great deal of surprise and disapproval.

"This place will do."

Facing each other the two men slowly backed away from one another each keeping their eyes firmly fixed upon the other. Simultaneously both stopped automatically adopting the stance of the gunfighter.

* * *

Gracie and Smith had one common trait. Neither was at their best during the morning. Both were night people. Rubbing sleep-filled eyes she joined him at the table. She'd worked out that in the days before his sight had failed Smith had been a cardsharp. Not that Smith ever talked about those days or Gracie ever asked. Employees at the Red Garter did not ask questions.

Today Smith was anxious to talk. He wanted a description of the Minister Reverend Clay Purnell. Gracie was happy to oblige.

"Well over six foot. Blond hair curling at the ends. He's a big man but all muscle. There ain't no fat on him." Luckily Smith couldn't see her smile. She ought to know about that considering she'd had a bird's-eye view. "Broad shoulders. Looks a mite like that outlaw Chivers. Are you feeling OK, Smith? You're looking a mite peculiar." She stopped chattering and eyed him curiously. "You ain't acquainted with our minister are you."

"No," he croaked unconvincingly. "And ain't likely to be. His kind don't come in the Red Garter."

"What do you want kid?" the bartender suddenly bawled. "It ain't laundry day."

For a dollar the kid toted the ladies' laundry to the Chinese laundry on Main Street and for a further dollar toted the clean clothes back. An arrangement that suited all concerned, the ladies maintaining they'd be damned before they toted laundry.

"Forget about the Goddamn laundry." The kid hopped with excitement. "Reverend Purnell's fixing to blast Dan Hater. Least he will if Dan Hater don't blast him first. That's worth a dime ain't it!"

Smith sent his coffee flying whilst Gracie and the bartender rushed for the batwings, the fat bartender bowling the scrawny kid over.

A fat hand clamped Gracie's neck.

"Women!" the bartender exclaimed in disgust. "Ain't got the sense of a hen. You rush out there, Gracie, and there's a good chance you'll take a stray slug. You can watch the show from here. Now quit wriggling. What in tarnation has got into Purnell? He'll need to be damn fast to down Hater."

Smith sat as though frozen but beads of sweat dotted his brow. He could have answered the bartender's question. Years back, in the good days he'd once saved a dirtbuster accused of rustling from being lynched. He'd faced down the whole town, made those organizing the necktie party back down. He'd done it for the hell of it and because he'd had a hunch the farmer was innocent.

Time had proved his hunch right.

And the man's name had been Purnell. There'd been two fair-headed kids, Smith recalled. Two beanpoles, thin limbs shooting out of threadbare clothes.

"God bless you, mister," the farmer had shouted. "Us Purnells never forget folk who do us a good turn."

"Or a bad one," a kid had yelled.

Smith believed the rancher who had organized the necktie party had died some time after that, caught afoot and run down by his own steers.

"Hush up now, Chivers," the older Purnell had said.

Smith began to pray, pray that Purnell wasn't just wearing an iron for show.

Outside on Main Street Clay kept his eyes fixed upon Hater's face totally ignoring the commotion on the sidewalks the two of them had caused. Folk had scattered for cover quicker than rabbits.

"Clay, don't do it," a woman's voice yelled.

"Gracie!" Clay's eyes remained fixed on Hater.

"See you in hell, Purnell." Even before he had finished speaking Hater's gunhand flashed downwards. But his eyes had betrayed his intention. Clay was ready. Simultaneously he also reached his hand closing over the cold butt of the heavy .45 hefting it fluidly, aiming and firing, firing to the left because he reckoned Hater would move to the left. Only a fool stood still.

Clay likewise moved to the left going down upon his knee as Hater's slug whistled past the spot Clay had been standing not a moment before. Desperately Clay triggered a second shot aiming for Dan Hater's chest, knowing he had to shoot to kill; if he did not he'd soon be a dead man; even wounded Hater would be lethal.

To his relief his slug took Hater fair and square in the chest. The bounty-hunter had been staring at Clay in disbelief.

Dan Hater didn't miss! Not ever!

And then Hater was keeling forward a dark stain spreading over the front of his shirt. Staggering to his feet Clay stumbled towards the man he had felled. With hands which were now not quite steady he turned Hater over to lie face upwards.

"It ain't too late to repent. Just think the words."

"Purnell!"

"Yes." Clay bent lower to catch the whispered last words of Dan Hater.

"You ain't suited to your job." Hater actually winked and then his head fell sideways.

Rising to his feet Clay stared down at the dead bounty-hunter. He'd also noted that every eye was fixed upon himself. He cussed silently. These folk were judging him. Their breed couldn't understand the way it had to be sometimes. Dan Hater had lived by the gun and died by the gun. And even dying the man had managed a quip. He'd gone out in style.

Clay squared his shoulders. A man paid his debts. But not for the first time he began to wonder whether Dan Hater's words were true. Was he suited to this line of work and if he wasn't why the hell had the Lord come to his rescue in his hour of need?

Not for the first time Clay found himself wishing he could go back to nursemaiding steers. They were preferable to people and that was a fact.

3

HE'D been in Wyoming territory when the event which had changed his way of life had occurred. Life was running smoothly. His pa had always wanted one of the boys to be a minister, for his pa was a religious man, but Chivers was robbing banks and Clay was herding cows. Both of them were a disappointment to that good man,

So, there he'd been in Wyoming territory, contriving to get there at the worst time of the year, and somehow or other he'd found himself separated from his two pards.

He had dismounted to put a steer with a broken leg out of its misery when his damn fool horse had elected to take off. Naturally, Clay had set off after the horse, it being reasonable to suppose it would, after a taste of freedom, stay put.

And then the snow had started, light at first but growing heavier, making it so that a man could not see where he was heading or where he'd come from. He'd fired off all of his shots, at decent spaced intervals, hoping that his pards would hear but there'd been no answering shots; no voices cussing him for being a damn fool.

He had faced the truth. Tonight he was going to die. It was impossible to survive. Exposure to the elements would surely kill him and he was damned if he wanted to die. He was in his prime and he was damned if he wanted to cross over to that place his pa kept spouting about.

He'd fought against the inevitable, struggling onwards, his eyes almost shot, his limbs almost numb. He'd halted, his vision obscured by snow and, instead of repenting of all the things he'd done which he ought not to have done, starting from the time he'd stolen a strip of candy from the general store, he'd started cussing and shaking his fist. What he said could not be repeated. But he had ended, "I ain't doing no repenting lest You give me a sign."

He'd then taken five steps forward and fallen over something more or less buried, a miracle to his uncomplicated way of looking at life. Of all things he'd stumbled over a freshly down bull buffalo, the corpse still warm. He'd known there was no time to lose for soon the snow would be coming in all its fury, this was just a taster of what was to come.

Drawing his knife with its keenly honed blade he'd slit open the belly of the dead animal pulling out handfuls of steaming entrails, making a place for himself inside that massive body. Then he'd gotten himself inside after wedging his Winchester upright between two rocks just in case another miracle occurred and his pards found the spot where he was buried.

And there he lay for an eternity in

his dark, odorous tomb the experience being enough to unhinge a man. He'd lapsed in and out of consciousness and when his pards had pulled him out, stiff as a board, but still breathing, he'd come round in time to hear the grizzled ramrod exclaim, "Hell, I don't know why the Lord has seen fit to spare you, Clay Purnell, but I reckon He must have a reason."

At the time Clay had thought he'd known what that reason might be but now as he stared down at the dead bounty-hunter doubts assailed him. He'd considered that he'd made a bargain and he had stuck to his bargain but why was it trouble seemed to follow him around?

And, as sure as hell, big trouble was coming to Capra. Trouble in the form of countless woollies. And he was stuck right in the middle of it. Hell, he guessed he'd have to put in for a transfer and hope he was away from the place before the woollies arrived. Some place peaceable, where there'd be no call for him to ever use his .45.

★ ★ ★

Slim Simpson hadn't given up hope of finding a place where his neighbours would allow him to live in peace. He was always the optimist and he'd grown weary of the killings; trouble had been dogging him it seemed all his life.

He'd been born a sheep man and now he reckoned he'd die one. And, throughout his years of herding sheep, he'd never been able to understand the strength of animosity just the sighting of a woolly was able to occasion in the most amicable of ranching men, or farming folk for that matter.

No one liked sheep herders. Even the law was known to turn a blind eye to the harassment which went on.

Electing to remain a sheep man had cost Slim dear. His long-suffering wife, unable to face the trouble which kept presenting itself and fearing for the young ones, had upped and left him. Slim couldn't blame her for it, for in his heart he knew she was better off with her sister back East, the piano teacher who'd never thought much of Slim.

And now before he could reach Capra and the land he'd bought Slim had one more hurdle to cross. He needed to stock up on supplies and his instincts, which had never let him down, informed him that there was a great deal of animosity in the two-bit town which stood between himself and Capra.

He'd done his best. He'd let it be known that he was only passing through but the ill-feeling had not abated. And now Slim, accompanied by one man, the rest of his Mexicans left to guard the flock, drove his wagon into town.

"You dirty stinking sheep man."

Out of the corner of his eye Slim had noted the troop of young ones following on behind his wagon. It had been one of the youngsters who had yelled out. Slim gritted his teeth and ignored the insult.

"You stink worse than your woollies!"

Slim evidenced no sign that he'd heard the remark. He'd heard them all before, many times. He also ignored the stones the youngsters snatched up and hurled after his wagon. Ignoring insults didn't come easy to Slim for he was not a man who believed there was any virtue in turning the other cheek. Do that and the assailant most likely would strike the other cheek. Also Slim's disposition was not mild. His temper was hot. Turning the other cheek did no good at all. All it did was to make folk think the *hombre* being attacked was yellow.

He climbed down from his wagon. Slim was his sobriquet for he was naturally long and thin, always looking in need of a good meal. His naturally sallow complexion implied that his state of health left much to be desired. His appearance fooled plenty and those who knew him knew better. In reality Slim Simpson was a tough as old leather and, when provoked, a dangerous man.

"Yah! My pa wouldn't even give you a job scaring the crows." The boy drew back his arm and let fly with a sharp-edged stone. Unfortunately his aim was good. The stone struck Slim on the temple drawing blood. As blood trickled down Slim's face, Manolito, Slim's hired man, held his breath. Slim's left eye was twitching, a warning sign. His temper was about to evidence itself.

"You stay put. I'll deal with this," Slim grunted. "That young one's got to learn that when he attacks an honest, hard-working, peaceable man, intent on minding his own business, well he's got to face the consequences."

"Sure boss," Manolito agreed.

Slim's long bony fingers closed over the handle of the bull whip. Slim always carried the whip. He reckoned it to be an ideal means of defence. But he also carried a concealed blade, his last resort when the sight of the whip failed to deter would-be assailants.

Slim spun round. The kid took to his heels. The whip cracked just once hitting the boy across the rump. Howling with pain the boy collapsed in the dirt. Slim re-coiled his whip and put it away, the sound of the boy's howling music to his ears. The other pesky young ones had bolted like rabbits. Now there wasn't a sign of one of them.

"I reckon that's learned him respect for his elders and betters," Slim observed. "You keep your eyes peeled for trouble whilst I deal with the storekeep!"

"*Si señor*," Manolito grinned. He'd been with Slim too many years. "And be damn quick about it!"

"I sure will," Slim replied. He didn't want trouble. Getting his stores and getting out of town pronto made damn good sense.

The storekeeper who'd been determined to tell the sheep man that he could get his supplies in hell had a change of heart for the sheep man now holding the bull whip loosely by the handle looked crazed, and any fool knew a bull whip could soon cut a man to ribbons.

Being a wise man the storekeeper smiled ingratiatingly. "Can I help you, mister?"

"Sure you can." Slim handed him the list. "Get these goods together and loaded into my wagon pretty damn quick."

"Sure mister." The storekeeper, surplus fat wobbling, hastened to oblige.

As the last sack of flour was heaved into the wagon, Manolito spoke up. "Trouble heading this way, boss."

"Damnation!" Slim squinted at the big man marching down Main Street. Years back Slim had seen a picture of a gorilla and this *hombre* with his hunched shoulders and long swinging arms put Slim in mind of a gorilla. And the gorilla's face had a striking resemblance to the face of the lad Slim had downed.

There was no sign of the boy. Slim had noted him crawling away on his hands and knees. Evidently the boy had crawled to his pa.

"Keep your rifle handy," Slim ordered, "and be ready to fork it out the instant I've finished dealing with this *hombre*."

"Sure thing, boss," Manolito agreed. On the sidewalks men were congregating. Their expressions, without exception, mean and eager. They put Manolito in mind of so many coyotes and if the boss went down the coyotes would launch their attack. He knew it. The boss knew it.

Slim managed a grin. "Quit fretting. I don't aim to be buried in this two-bit town!" He spat contemptuously, and raised his voice. "Hold it right there, farmer. I done your lad a favour. Another man would have shot him. And don't you be discounting the fact that if it had been a mite lower that stone could have left me blind in one eye." But the words didn't register.

"You hurt my boy. Hurt him real bad. He'll be laid up for weeks."

"The boy got what he deserved."

"Damn stinking sheep herder." The giant grinned in anticipation revealing a mouth filled with yellow teeth. "I'm going to feed your eyes, both of them, to my pigs. It'll take more than a damn whip to stop me." There was a feral light in his eyes.

"Damnation," Slim swore again. The fellow had the strength of a bull and the brains of a chicken: wasn't it obvious that he could not wait to be cut down, stomped badly and maybe fed to the hogs? Wasn't it obvious he had to save himself?

And wasn't there only one way he could save himself? The bull whip could stop most of them but it wouldn't stop this one.

Slim stooped, going down into a crouch and, straightening his wrist going back, the blade he pulled out of his boot flew through the air before folk even realized his intention. With a sickening thud, the nine-inch sharply honed blade thudded into its target, the farmer's broad forehead.

Slow moving, slow thinking; the farmer, after declaring his intentions, had been as good as dead. No way would Slim Simpson end up as hog food.

Even as the man hit the ground Slim was rushing forward to retrieve his blade. And, even as Manolito cracked the reins, Slim was running after the wagon, tumbling into the back of it as the vehicle gathered speed.

"You reckon they'll come after us?"

Slim pondered the question. "Nope. Might have done if he'd been a ranching man. But farmers are a different breed. More cautious. Less backbone."

"Yellow!"

"That one weren't," Slim corrected. "Would have been better for him if he had been." He cut himself a slab of baccy and chewed thoughtfully. His conscience was clear. He'd only done what he had to do. There'd been no other way.

* * *

"There's no other way," Mrs Brewes declared sanctimoniously. "That man has got to go. Why, he's a disgrace to his calling. A drunkard and a killer. And" — here she lowered her voice — "and immoral. Don't you agree Husband."

John Brewes had little patience with his wife. "Hell, woman, are you suggesting I ride into Capra and shoot the minister?"

"John Brewes how dare you say such a thing. We're Christian folk."

"Then quit yapping. I've got wide-loopers to deal with, not to mention the stinking woollies on the way to ruin the range. Not to mention a lawman fool enough to allow himself to be gunned down by a deranged wife. The Lord knows when Gaskill will be up and about fit to do his job. The honest truth is I don't give a damn about the Reverend Purnell. I've got more important matters on my mind. If he wants to share a jug with that old coot at the livery barn that's all right by me. And we all know Dan Hater was a no-account bounty-hunter! If Purnell is busy sniffing round that female at the Red Garter leastways it might stop him concerning himself with matters which ain't none of his concern. Now, out of my way. I've got to do what's got to be done." He paused. "There ain't no other way."

Angrily Mrs Brewes watched her husband and his men ride out. She was not in the least concerned about the men John Brewes intended to hang. She never spared them a thought. All she could think about was the Reverend Clay Purnell. The good ladies of Capra were rightly outraged. They were looking to her to find a way to get rid of the man. She couldn't let them down.

4

"REVEREND PURNELL!"

Swinging around Clay found himself grinning foolishly at the two people who had just stepped out of the Red Garter. One of them was Childs, Smith as he was now, and the other was Gracie. She'd stayed silent. Smith was the one who'd spoken up.

"That's me," Clay rejoined. "Howdy there, Gracie. Care to join me on a picnic next Sunday? I'll fix up the food and call by for you around ten say."

She eyed him speculatively managing to hide her surprise. "A picnic, well, I never. You're full of surprises." Her eyes narrowed. "Don't the trouble you're in bother you none? I heard tell last Sunday you were preaching to an empty church; I've also heard tell that next Sunday the ladies aim to march up and down with placards.

You're occasioning a good deal of mirth in this town, Clay. Leastways inside the saloons."

"Let them." He almost said to hell with the ladies of Capra. "What about the picnic? Say yes."

"Maybe. I'll think on it." She flounced inside.

Clay turned his attention to Smith. "It ain't necessary to thank me. I'll get my reward in the hereafter."

"Just have a mind you don't get it before then," Smith replied drily. "And thanks all the same. I know why you killed Dan Hater."

"You want to thank me then show up one Sunday. A man feels plain foolish talking to himself. I can't cotton what's gotten into those folk. Sure I killed Hater but it was done fair."

"It ain't Hater's death that's put the womenfolk against you. You're showing a bit too much interest in Gracie. It ain't done. Your predecessor now, well, he weren't all they thought him to be. He was a man who appreciated the value of subterfuge."

"I ain't with you."

"Damn it man, your predecessor, well, every now and again he'd sneak into the Red Garter, up the backstairs, pay his money and enjoy a little female companionship without none being the wiser. He had an arrangement with the boss you see. Cost him extra but he reckoned it was worth it. But what do you do? Ask Gracie to go on a picnic. The whole town will see you ride out."

"The way you're suggesting ain't my way," Clay rejoined.

"I guess I ought to be glad you're a damn fool." Smith shrugged his shoulders. "Only a damn fool would have taken on Dan Hater. You just have a care now, do you hear, a care that you don't find yourself taking on the whole town."

Clay grinned for all that Smith could not see the grin. "Right now I aim to shake the dust of Capra off my boots. Fact is I can't abide town living. That's my problem. I aim to take me a ride. A darn long one. See you around. Leastways I expect you to show up one Sunday."

"You can keep expecting," Smith joked. "Hell will freeze over before I put foot inside your church. And Purnell, whilst you're taking your ride just try and stay out of trouble. You're in deep enough. No point in wading in deeper."

Whistling cheerfully, his thoughts turning upon the picnic Clay headed for the livery barn. He liked what he'd seen of Gracie and he reckoned she'd liked what she'd seen of him. And she'd seen a good deal. Taking that swim had been the best thing he'd done in a long while.

* * *

There were two of them in the crude dugout, an old man and one who was not much more than a boy.

The old-timer's name was Possum a

sobriquet well earned. Once years back he'd escaped the jaws of an irate grizzly by playing dead. Now Possum, chewing at a plug of baccy, watched tolerantly whilst the kid worked at perfecting a fast draw. To the kid this was all an adventure still.

The kid liked to talk whilst old Possum was dour of feature and taciturn by nature. Surprisingly the two got on real well.

"First thing I aim to do is buy me a pair of handsome boots," the kid declared, "and maybe a Stetson. And a new Spencer Carbine."

Possum hid a grin. The kid had yet to get around to women. "Quit yapping kid," he rejoined good-naturedly. "It's your turn to cook. And this time don't burn the steak nor the biscuits. I've got a strong constitution but it can only take so much. Get moving. My belly tells me it's time to eat."

"Sure thing." The kid grinned. Actually it was Possum's turn to cook but the oldster seized every opportunity to weasel out of that particular chore.

* * *

John Brewes squinted up at the sky. He noted a buzzard or two and grinned. If the birds stayed around they'd soon have plenty to fill their bellies with. With a grunt he wiped away the sweat which beaded his brow. "Sure is hot," he observed.

"Hotter than hell," Parkin rejoined cheerfully. Heat never seemed to bother Parkin none. "And that's where those darn wideloopers will be headed. All thanks to my sharp eyes."

It had been Parkin who had found the hideout. The talk about his sharp eyes was just his way of reminding Brewes that when the wideloopers had been despatched there was a handsome bonus to be collected. Not that Mr Brewes was liable to forget. Mr Brewes was a man with a long memory as many had found out to their cost.

"Damn polecats," Brewes snarled. He pointed at one of the hands. "You stay with the horses. Any sign of trouble coming you fire a warning shot. You hear now."

"Sure thing Mr Brewes."

Drawing his .45 Brewes, on foot, led the way into the narrow, all-but-concealed passageway, a passageway gouged out of the rock by time, wide enough for one horse but not two abreast.

"If we don't get them forget the bonus," Brewes warned. "I want the polecats themselves not just the steers they've lifted."

"Leastways you'll get the beef, Mr Brewes," a hand observed. Plainly they could all hear the sound of the penned-up cattle.

The dugout lay below them now. There was no sign of life, no sign of a look-out but a thin wisp of grey smoke headed upwards told them that the dugout was in use. Behind the dugout they could see the holding pens containing cattle which wore Brewes' brand. About 200 of them. Not that that made a difference. A man hanged whether he stole one cow or 200 of them.

"I only see two horses!" Brewes scowled at Parkin. "You told me there was at least a dozen of them holed-up here."

"So there was. Then." Parkin hadn't exactly investigated the passageway, just read the tracks.

"Boys, if it's humanly possible I want those two polecats inside taken alive!" Brewes' thoughts were plain ugly. There was no such thing as honour amongst thieves. Once he got to work the polecats would soon tell him all there was to tell. He'd planned to leave a dozen of them dangling. The fact that there seemed to be only two sure stuck in his craw.

The hand who'd been left minding the horses was an *hombre* answering to the name of Larkin. When the rider appeared Larkin's first thought was to blast him out of the saddle and he would have done had it not been for the black suit and stiff white collar.

Seeing the minister approaching Larkin had no thought of firing a warning shot. In fact he grinned amicably. Reverend Purnell was in time to say a word or two over the soon-to-be if not-yet-dead polecats. Larkin couldn't see how Brewes could reasonably object to this.

Larkin grinned broadly. "Howdy there, Reverend Purnell."

"Mind telling me what's afoot?" Clay enquired. If he'd not been the minister Larkin quite naturally would have told him to go to hell but a clerical garb had the most amazing effect as Clay had soon discovered.

Larkin was only too happy to oblige. "Have you brought the Good Book along?" Larkin concluded. "Sure as hell you'll be needing it, begging your pardon Reverend."

Clay tapped his pocket. "Never ride out without it. If you've no objection

I'll be getting where I'm needed." He winked at Larkin. "Even the dead need praying for." He hoped he would get there in time. Maybe Brewes had already strung them up. The gunfire which had been audible but a moment ago had abruptly concluded.

"You go right ahead." Larkin puffed out his chest. Without further palaver Clay dug in his heels glad he'd not had to fight his way in. Words worked damn well. Sometimes. But words wouldn't work on John Brewes.

* * *

"Damn tough this steak." Possum laboured with his knife. "You ain't put enough lard in the pan. I like my meat well cooked. When a man gets on in years chewing comes harder. You'll learn that one day, kid. Try and remember next time."

"Sure will." The kid chewed away, That had been one of the longest sentences old Possum had strung together. The kid was wise enough not to grin. Next thing he'd know he'd be feeling the pan connecting with his head. Despite the toughness of the steak the two chewed away with enthusiasm.

They were still chewing when the door was kicked open. Possum, reaching for his ancient buffalo gun, took a slug in the shoulder. And they then found themselves surrounded by a ring of guns.

"Looks like we've come to the end of the trail, kid," Possum observed as he spread a hand over his bleeding shoulder. He wanted to let the kid know what was in store for them, prepare him so that when the kid saw the hanging ropes he could acquit himself with dignity. The kid was untried. Possum hoped he would not shame himself by grovelling, by begging; it would all be to no avail for the words would fall upon deaf ears.

It was John Brewes himself who had them.

To his credit the kid kept his lips buttoned other than to mutter, "I reckon."

"Get them outside," Brewes snarled. Right now Brewes put old Possum in mind of a mad dog or outraged grizzly. Both were lethal. Looking up at the sky the old man reflected it was as good a day as any to die. And die they would. Hanged forthwith for that was how it was done.

John Brewes glowered at his two captives. What a haul. A kid and an old man. Hell! He spat contemptuously.

"Let me tell you two varmints the kind of man you're dealing with. I'm a man who, when he sets out to do a job, does a darn good job. I came up from Texas in '76 battling the elements all the way. I ain't worked, slaved all these years to let bastards like you and your kind rob me blind. You two weren't alone. Where's the rest of your gang? I aim to see the lot of you planted six feet under."

Possum managed a wry smile. "It

ain't your lucky day Mr Brewes. Two you've got and two is all you're having. Hell will freeze over before I rat on my pards and it ain't no use you questioning the kid, he's on approval. He ain't privy to all the information. He doesn't know. So quit gabbing. Get on with it. Hang us high, that's your intention ain't it?"

"It sure as hell is," Brewes snarled. "Make no mistake about that, old man. You're going to die but before you do you're going to tell me what I want to know.

"Don't bet on it," Possum rejoined.

Brewes' grin was feral. His look poison. "I ain't a betting man. My hands will vouch for that."

"Better tell Mr Brewes what he wants to know," Parkin advised. "You will in the end."

"No."

"Parkin get that damn kindling. Want to change your mind, old-timer? Not yet? But you will. I promise you."

Clay dug in his heels. The passageway twisted in places, he had yet to see light but the howl of pain from somewhere up ahead told him he was needed and pretty damn quick.

"For God's sake, Possum, tell them," the shouted words momentarily rose above the howls.

Unsheathing his rifle Clay came out of the passageway cursing as his gaze took in the scene below. A scene from hell being enacted before his very eyes, except that instead of devils Brewes and his crew could be substituted. Clay descended the gradient recklessly without regard to his own safety or the safety of his horse. Fortunately the animal was sure-footed.

The men below just gazed at him. They knew him, leastways by sight. Accustomed to the ineffectual harmless wool-gathering *hombre* who'd been Clay's predecessor, they for the most part expected nothing more than a ear bashing.

Clay levelled his rifle. "Pull him back

or so help me, Brewes, I'll blast you where you stand."

Parkin without waiting to be told pulled the old man away from the fire. The oldster's feet were blistered and peeling, the skin beneath like raw meat. A tough old coot, Parkin thought, with grudging respect. He hadn't blabbed although whether the oldster could have continued to hold out, why that wasn't something Parkin would have cared to bet on. Secretly Parkin was glad it was over. A quick clean lynching was one thing. This was another matter entirely and Brewes ought to be damn well ashamed of himself.

"Easy boys," Parkin advised. "We don't want to see the boss blasted." But we want an end to this torture. Wisely he kept those thoughts to himself.

John Brewes narrowed his eyes. He recognized that Purnell was crazy enough to shoot. Also lawmen and men of the cloth, well, they were a special breed, killing one of them could stir up a hornets' nest. Brewes didn't want to be known as the man who'd gunned down the minister. That tag would stick for evermore, dog him for years.

"All the old coot needed to do was tell me where the rest of the gang is hanging out," Brewes declared self-righteously. "The old fool brought this upon himself and that's a fact."

Clay nodded. "It's over now."

Brewes shrugged. "I'll not argue with you, Purnell, for I can see you sincerely believe you've got right on your side. OK, boys, the fun is over. String up those polecats. You're welcome to pray with them first, Minister, or after it's done I'll not hinder you in the performance of your duty."

"That man will be crippled for life."

Brewes raised a brow in surprise. "That ain't a problem seeing he ain't got much life left."

Parkin opened his mouth to speak, thought better of it and clamped his lips together. Brewes ought to have set to work on the young one. The oldster would have spoken up quick enough then to save his young pard. But Parkin had learned not to offer words of advice. Brewes would only have told him to shut his mouth, reminded him he was paid to obey orders not to think. That was the boss's way. Eyeing the new minister speculatively Parkin decided the man was trouble, big trouble; like the boss, Clay Purnell was a man of decided views.

The kid, clearly afraid and fighting to control his fear, glared defiantly at Clay. "You go to hell, Minister. I don't need no praying from you."

Clay ignored the kid. He concentrated on Brewes. "What you ought to have done was take those two men into town. Put them in jail. Held them until the judge showed up and tried them fair and square. The way I see it you've already judged them and decided their punishment yourself. These two *hombres* have had their punishment. The oldster has been tortured whilst the kid's been forced to watch. You ain't punishing them twice. Once is enough."

"What the hell are you saying?" Brewes demanded. Clay Purnell was a case for the asylum.

"That you ain't going to hang them. You've learned them a lesson. Now you're letting them go!"

"The hell I am!"

"We've reached an impasse, Mr Brewes," Clay explained patiently. "Of course you can gun me down but I'm betting I can blast you before I take a slug." He played his trump card. "I was sent here, directed here if you like, for a purpose. To save these two polecats. The Lord doesn't want to see them yet awhile."

"You're mad," Brewes spat. "And there's only one thing saving you from the hereafter. Damn it I was raised to respect a minister and the thought of gunning one down goes against all I believe."

Not to mention the fact that awkward

questions could be asked.

"My men are decent men," Brewes continued. "I can't ask them to gun down a man of God so we'll do things your way this time, Purnell. Mount up boys and get those steers out of here."

"You've done right, Mr Brewes," a veteran hand declared.

"Yeah," Brewes rejoined sourly. Clay Purnell either had to be transferred by his superiors or else he had to meet with an accident. Capra wasn't big enough for both of them. Brewes began to turn over ways in his mind, ways of ridding himself of the meddlesome minister.

Possum propped himself up on his elbows. The pain was excruciating. Now he knew what hell must be like. John Brewes was actually riding out. "Why?" he gasped.

"Us ministers have a special place in the community," Clay rejoined. "If Brewes wants to keep the town's respect he can't gun me down, leastways not openly. Folk don't like me but by killing me Brewes would turn them against him. He's too damn smart to make a wrong move. I gambled on it and won this time." He eyed the kid. "Help me get the oldster inside. We'll do what we can for those feet which ain't much."

He hefted his saddle-bag over one shoulder. Providently he had ointment with him. He never travelled without a small vial of carbolic acid, a powerful antiseptic he reckoned, a knitting needle and a pair of pincers plus a fiddle string and needle. Just having those things meant the difference between life and death. On every trail drive there was always one of the men who'd turned his hand to doctoring, and on every drive Clay had been on he'd been the one given that unenviable job. Some he'd saved. Some he'd lost. But the oldster was as tough as dried leather. Clay reckoned he'd pull through.

5

IF a look could kill Clay knew he'd drop dead. Slapping down his plate of pie with scarcely concealed fury she eyed him viciously.

"Hope you enjoyed your picnic, Reverend Purnell!" She sniffed disapprovingly. "Can't say your predecessor neglected his duties to go off picnicking."

"Maybe not," Clay rejoined. He could have told her a few tales about his predecessor which would have made her hair stand on end. He grinned, unable to hide his amusement.

"You were gone a mighty long time," she stated, folding her arms across her scrawny chest.

"I sure was." He forked in a mouthful of pie his eyes straying beyond the woman to the sidewalk opposite her eating-house. "Anything in particular you want to know?"

"Certainly not." She bolted for the kitchen bristling with indignation. The Lord only knew what that shameless man would say next.

Peering through the grimy glass Clay watched as the ramrod Parkin worked his way down Main Street entering every establishment with the exception of the dressmaker's. Trouble, Clay thought, as he chewed his apple pie. Parkin was spreading the word, the word according to John Brewes, and Clay didn't even have to guess what the word might be. He knew.

"How much do I owe you." He finished his coffee.

"Reverend Purnell!" She twisted her apron nervously occasioning Clay to look at her questioningly.

"Yes."

"In future," she spoke hurriedly, almost tripping oyer the words, "I'll thank you to stay out of my restaurant; this is a respectable place for respectable people."

Clay shrugged. "Sure. I'll be happy

to stay out of your restaurant. Your pastry wasn't cooked right. Reckon you took that pie out of the oven too soon." He sauntered out enjoying the gasp of outraged indignation his words occasioned. He'd been lying. Her pastry had been cooked just fine.

Luckily his disposition was even. When folk turned against him he never let it get to him. He dismissed the fool woman from his mind and strolled towards the nearest general store.

Whistling cheerfully he entered the interior enjoying the smell of coffee, soap, bacon, dried apples; a general store sold just about everything from pins to a portable house. The man behind the counter was huge, he sat complacently, hands folded oyer a massive paunch.

"Howdy there, Reverend Purnell." A chuckle shook the massive frame. "Things have sure hotted up since your arrival in town. Worst thing that ever happened hereabouts was that every now and then an *hombre* would be caught fishing on the Lord's day. Things sure is different ain't they!" He eyed Clay expectantly.

"That ain't my doing," Clay rejoined.

"Yes sir," the storekeeper continued, "John Brewes has political ambitions. Didn't know that did you? I reckon those ambitions saved your hide. Hell, what possessed you to turn those widelopers free?"

Clay shrugged. "What did Parkin want?" He ignored the fool question.

"Not a damn thing excepting to give me a few words of advice. John Brewes ain't going to be kindly disposed towards anyone in this town who has truck with those stinking sheep men."

"What did you say?" Clay reckoned he knew the answer.

"First off no threats were needed. I've already written out my sign." He held up a wooden board and burnt upon it were the words Clay had feared to see. *No sheep men served*. "That I ain't so desperate that I need sell my goods to sheep men. And I can tell you now this town is in one mind about it. You don't look too happy, Reverend Purnell!"

"Well, I reckoned it was too much to expect to find one sane and reasonable man in this two-bit town," Clay rejoined, his expression sour. Folk always brought trouble upon themselves. Capra was no exception.

"Enjoy your picnic, Reverend?" the storekeeper enquired slyly.

Clay shrugged.

"Did you?" The man leered suggestively. "You know what I mean!"

"If you're looking to keep your teeth, keep your nose out of what don't concern you," Clay grated angrily.

"No offence intended." The storekeeper remained unabashed. "Good luck to you I say. Leastways you're giving those old hens something to talk about. I get them in here every day spending an hour or more fingering a length of gingham then deciding not to buy."

Clay stomped out. His request to be found another town had been turned down. He'd been advised to let the law deal with any trouble which reared its head.

Gaskill was healing, albeit slowly. Clay found the sheriff sitting up in bed. The first thing that struck a man about Gaskill was the fact that the sheriff possessed eyes as cold and unblinking as a fish. Eyes that had made many an *hombre* lose his nerve when facing up to Gaskill. There was no hint of warmth in the man. Clay decided that Gaskill was a man who didn't give a damn about anything save the size of his pay cheque. But here Clay found he had misjudged the man.

"Howdy there, Reverend," Gaskill greeted him with at least a hint of warmth. "I guess I owe you a word of thanks," he continued awkwardly, thanking didn't come easy to Gaskill. "I hear tell this two-bit town was planning to lynch Mrs Gaskill and would have done so if you had not intervened."

Clay shrugged diffidently. "It ain't

my way to watch a woman hang," he rejoined. He smiled drily, "In Mrs Gaskill's case I reckon she was driven to it; mitigating circumstances I reckon."

"You're damn right," surprisingly Gaskill agreed.

"Are you going to press charges?" Clay enquired. "It could mean the asylum!"

"Hell no." Gaskill was clearly outraged at the notion. "I love my wife." Embarrassed at having betrayed a weakness he asked quickly, "What brings you here, Reverend?"

"Are you going to side with Brewes against the sheep herders?" Clay demanded, without preamble. "That's why he brought you here ain't it, a loaded gun to aim at the sheep men?"

"Sure." Gaskill smirked. "And paying me handsome he is too."

"Yes or no," Clay persisted.

"Things have changed now," Gaskill responded slowly.

"How so?"

"I hear tell Brewes was ready to stand idle whilst Mrs Gaskill was lynched."

"You're quitting?" Clay asked in disbelief.

"Hell no. I aim to draw my salary. When trouble erupts, as it will, the polecats can fight it out amongst themselves. The more of them that gets gunned down the better. With luck Brewes could take a slug and that will be the end of it. He's the driving force in this town. Without Brewes the rest of them will mutter and curse but they'll not make a stand against the sheep men. What's your concern? Don't tell me your aim is to save lives as well as souls. Well, I can tell you how to save a whole bundle of lives."

"How? The army won't get involved in this until the trouble is well under way."

"Hell, I ain't talking about the army. Are you a fool, Purnell? The answer is staring you plain in the face. Take out Brewes. I don't give a damn.

Sure as hell I won't be investigating if Brewes meets up with an accident. And I'll see no one else does either. I owe you that." He winked. "I'm an uncomplicated man, Reverend, with a simple view of life. It's the best way. Saves a whole heap of trouble."

Clay shook his head. "I won't be taking out Brewes. And" — here he paused — "and if John Brewes meets up with an accident you might not be asking questions but I will. Questions concerning your whereabouts at the time of the accident."

"Don't mistake me, I ain't offering to kill the man for you," Gaskill rejoined, "I'm just telling you the way to do it. And it's got to be done before the woollies arrive. You think on it." Gaskill was clearly unperturbed. "Leastways have a care that conscience of yours doesn't get you blasted. I'm betting John Brewes is already working on ways to get rid of you."

"Maybe," Clay agreed. Brewes had behaved out of character backing down without a fight. Clay was uneasy.

On the way out Clay met Doc and from the way Doc dropped his eyes, kind of ashamed, Clay knew he had agreed to go along with Brewes' suggestion; wounded sheep men were not to be treated.

Angrily Clay rounded on him. "Don't you even think of refusing to treat a injured sheep herder. You took an oath to save life and I aim to see that you honour that oath. Turn them away and you'll have me to deal with." The door slammed in Clay's wake.

Doc scratched his bald head. Thoughtfully he stared at the closed door. He'd surely like to know what had gone on during that picnic. The Reverend Purnell and Gracie — his wife was harping on about it something chronic. As far as the womenfolk were concerned there was only one subject worth discussing these days and it wasn't sheep herders.

* * *

"Heh Minister!"

Clay turned round. He recognized the girl although he did not know her name. She was from the Red Garter, a mite younger than Gracie and not nearly so snappy. Bad temper he reckoned came with the years spent in their particular line of work.

"Can I help you ma'am?" he enquired. Leastways someone was speaking to him.

At that she giggled. "Nope. But I can help you. Gracie sent me, on account of she didn't want to embarrass you by seeking you out in Main Street. Folk in this town are watching every move you two make. Leastways the ladies!"

Clay nodded. "I reckon."

"You'd best stay out of your house tonight," the girl advised. She giggled again. "We all think highly of you at the saloon. Us girls wouldn't like to see you burnt to a crisp." She shrugged. "Putting it plainly, certain drunken bums have been making plans to burn you out. Tonight's the night."

She winked. "You've got a choice, Clay, stay and shoot it out or join Gracie at the Red Garter. We'll leave the door open; you can sneak in by way of the backstairs. I wouldn't advise you to turn Gracie down on account of the fact that she's liable to shoot you herself if you prefer gunplay to her companionship." Swinging her hips she sauntered off leaving Clay staring after her.

A night attack. He hadn't reckoned on the polecats wanting to try their hand at burning him out. Hell, he'd learn them. Leastways the man he had been would have learned them. The old Clay Purnell would not have balked at gunplay. Even now he'd be thinking of ways to outgun those murderously inclined polecats. Clay groaned. The Reverend Clay Purnell, however, was duty bound to avoid the taking of life. If he fought them off as he was inclined to do it was very likely one or more of the polecats would end up dead.

He considered his situation. A grin

spread over his face. Gracie's invitation had been issued to keep him away from gunplay. She couldn't want to see him shot. And an unexpected and tempting offer it was. He'd be a fool to turn her down. The house was not even his own, it went with the job. It belonged to the town.

The girl had not said who was behind this. He guessed Gracie did not want him to know. It was the best way for he knew that if he'd been given names he might have given in to the temptation to seek them out.

Saving those two wideloopers had cost him dear but considering how Brewes had behaved Clay didn't have any regrets. John Brewes had been having his way around here for too damn long. There was darn little decency left in the man. Brewes might be behind this, or he might not. But Brewes would sure as hell know about it. And Brewes, with but one word, would have been able to stop it.

He made his decision. He was going

to Gracie and to hell with the lot of them. And maybe, just maybe, it was all wild talk, drunken bums out to impress whoever might be listening.

* * *

They struck around two in the morning. Lying in the dark, dozing, Clay was awoken by a sharp elbow dug in his side.

"What did I tell you," she hissed. "I was right all along." In a flash she was at the window, eager to see. He joined her. From the window they could see the red glow of fire. And they heard the loud whoops of glee accompanied by a triumphant volley of shots.

There were six of them he observed as the mounted figures raced down Main Street disappearing into the darkness. If he'd been of a mind he could have felled at least two of them, knocked them out of the saddle as they deserved but he had known he could not do it, shoot them dead one day and preach over the graves the next. He frowned. He could not fight back. His hands were effectively tied.

The fire bell continued to peal out but the street remained deserted.

"Goddamnit!" Gracie swore explicitly. "There ain't one of them turned out to save you."

Clay grinned. "It's a mite late in the day for saving ain't it Gracie?" he observed.

"Well they ought to have tried." She was angry on his behalf. "Hell, Clay, you made a whole parcel of enemies throwing in with those widcloopers and being seen with me ain't helped you none!"

"I'm my own man," he rejoined. "It ain't my way to go around striving to please other folks."

"Clay!"

"Yup."

"It's spread. The church has taken alight. Now that'll get them moving." She softened her voice. "I'm truly sorry, Clay, I know how pained you must be feeling."

At that he almost laughed. "Hell, Gracie, I ain't feeling pained. I'm thankful that I ain't burning along with the house and church." He paused. "Women get the darnest ideas and that's a fact."

He peered out of the window. Men were moving now. And womenfolk likewise running to save the church they'd worked so hard at building. Clay shrugged. There was no hope of that for they'd delayed too long. He turned away from the window, "I guess I'll stay here, leastways until morning. I can't stomach the sight of setting eyes on any of them right now." He grinned. "Let them think I'm dead until tomorrow. When they learn different, well, some of those faces will be worth seeing."

6

SLIM SIMPSON brought his flock to a halt. Approaching, coming in fast, was Manolito. Always cautious Slim had sent Manolito on ahead to spy out the lie of the land. More than once this precautionary measure had stopped them leading his sheep into a trap. And now Manolito was back, waving his sombrero, the signal that the flock must stop moving forward.

Manolito's long, miserable-looking face had never been known to show much emotion but now Slim could see that Manolito was plainly excited. Leaning back in the saddle, Slim stretched his muscles for his back ached something chronic. With the back of his hand he wiped his sweating, dust-begrimed face.

"Hotter than hell," he muttered,

puzzled as to what this could be all about, for Manolito was clearly excited as opposed to being afraid or concerned.

"A good day for us all, Señor Slim," Manolito declared, coming to a halt before his boss. He grinned, expansively white teeth flashing.

"How's that," Slim grunted. "Don't tell me you've run into folk with a welcoming smile upon their faces." He guffawed at his own jest.

Manolito's smile broadened as he responded, "Without doubt, Señor Slim, if luck favours us we will see many welcoming smiles."

"Now that hardly makes sense," Slim observed, his interest aroused. "Since when have folk been glad to see woollies!"

"Ah but they'll like the sight of the bank robber Chivers, caught and bound, brought to face justice." Manolito frowned. "Ah, I forget, the poster say dead or alive."

"Chivers!" Slim exclaimed his

excitement rising. "You've come across Chivers!" As the bank robber's audacity had grown so had the reward. Quickly Slim did some mental arithmetic. There were ten of them, himself and Manolito and eight other Mexican herders, split the reward money ten ways and it was still a sum to risk dying for.

Manolito nodded. "By chance I discovered them. There is a small watering-hole up ahead, no more than a muddied puddle but water nevertheless. There I saw Chivers and five of his men all of them sprawled upon the ground in a state of exhaustion. One is wounded!"

For a long while there was silence as Slim chewed his plug of tobacco. Finally he obscrved, "I guess we'll take a vote on what to do. I won't force anyone to risk his hide getting Chivers."

Manolito shrugged. "There is no risk *señor*. We can come upon them unobserved and gun them down before they realize their danger. They have not posted a guard!"

Slim nodded. "We'll still vote. That's my way of doing things." And the less that participate the more that there will be to share out he thought silently. He therefore gave his men no encouragement but nevertheless they all unanimously decided they'd take their chance.

"And don't none of you gun down that bastard Chivers," Slim ordered.

"Why?" Manolito frowned.

"Because I say so," Slim snapped, unwilling to reveal that he was vain enough to want the pleasure of dragging Chivers into town at the end of a rope. Damnit for once in his life he wanted to hear congratulations instead of curses; for one time he did not want to be the outsider, let Chivers be the despised outsider.

"It would be safer to kill him for the man is poison," Manolito cautioned.

"No, we do it my way." Slim thought a moment and then forced a grin, "It ain't like you to turn down a good time, Manolito. We'll take him into town, claim the reward and then stay around and watch the hanging. That'll give you men time to get your fill of whiskey and willing women." He winked. "I can't think of a better way of spending the reward."

A volley of whoops greeted this announcement. Manolito knew that the men were with Slim on this but nevertheless tried to make them see sense one last time. "Chivers I hear tell he never forgets those who do him a bad turn."

"Hell, I ain't worried about Chivers seeking vengeance. By the time we get him to town he'll be no threat; he ain't special, just an ordinary *hombre*. He can't walk through bars."

Manolito kept silent. It could be that Señor Simpson was making one hell of a mistake. Maybe. But the boss's ears were closed to reason.

* * *

Carefully Chivers trickled water between the wounded man's parched lips. Goddamnit he cursed silently, their luck had all but run out. Sure they'd lost the posse which had been dogging their trail but they were all but out of ammunition, food and water. Their horses were all but worn out and, for the first time in his career as an owlhoot, Chivers was unsure of his next move.

And, as always, the men were looking to him for leadership.

"What will we do boss?" one of them asked.

Staring at Tom's worried face Chivers searched for words to give the man hope but then, before he could frame a reply, Tom's face exploded fragmenting into blood and gore spattering over Chivers.

He grabbed up his own rifle knowing the hopelessness of it for he only had two slugs left. Goddamnit the posse had succeeded in running them down and here he'd been congratulating himself on having outfoxed them. And he'd made the mistake of camping down on low ground. They were sitting ducks. Done for.

All around him bullets were thudding into his four men even when they were down and still upon the ground. But not him. Nothing hit him. Purposely for they were not aiming at him. Someone wanted him alive. Not the men for they were small fish. He was the big one. But why? It made no difference. The reward was the same be he brought in dead or alive.

And then there was a sudden abrupt silence. Bodies lay around him, all of them dead, shot down without a chance to surrender.

"Show yourself you bastards," he yelled, mad with rage and grief for the ones who had died had all been friends.

"Put down that rifle or we'll blast you."

"Blast away," he yelled defiantly, "for I don't give a damn!"

"He's crazy." Slim reached for his hat which had fallen from his head, "Crazy and trigger happy!"

The instant the hat showed itself Chivers blasted it without thinking, realizing only after the bullet had been wasted that he'd fallen for the oldest trick there was, the hat upon a stick.

"Goddamnit!" He threw the rifle from him for he'd thought up a trick of his own.

"He's out of shells," Slim grunted. "What did I tell you, Manolito? I told you it would be damn easy. Let's get him roped."

"*Si señor*." Manolito took the words to be a direct order. He took up his lariat, rose to his feet, beckoned to the men to help him subdue the owlhoot if necessary and started downwards towards the defeated, beaten man.

Chivers knowing he had but the moment moved with speed desperately snatching up his rifle and levelling it at the man he took to be the boss, the lead man toting the rope. He whooped with exultation as his last shot hit home.

Manolito staggered back, a dull red stain spreading across the middle of his spotless white tunic. He clutched the wound knowing that he was going to die on account of Slim Simpson's foolishness.

"Take him alive," Slim yelled. They'd scattered momentarily but when no more shots followed he knew that now the owlhoot really had run out of ammunition. "Use the rifle butts but don't kill him." Stricken he knelt beside the dying man. They'd been together a long time. Surprisingly Slim felt no remorse, for he'd never been one to blame himself for misfortune. He lowered his head to catch Manolito's painful whisper. And then jerked away as if he'd been shot himself.

"Damn you for a fool, Slim." The words were barely audible but Slim heard them sure enough. Manolito's eyes glazed, his head fell to one side and with a shudder he died.

Slim rose to his feet. His way of thinking remained unchanged. The bastard would go in alive. He would sweat it out in a stinking bug-infested cell until the day they took him out, paraded him before the town, mounted him upon a platform and kicked the stool away from beneath him and if the rope had been fixed right then Chivers would be a long time strangling.

He ran towards the scene below. Chivers was down and taking a pounding from the rifle butts not to mention booted feet. Reaching his men Slim had to bodily haul them away from the near unconscious owlhoot. One look at the man told Slim that no way could Chivers be dragged into town at the end of the rope. There was nothing for it but to throw the man into the wagon and hope he made it into town without expiring upon the way.

* * *

John Brewes vented his rage and frustration upon his hapless ramrod Parkin.

Previously his mood had been good-humoured and also a trifle guilty, guilty that he had not said the words to stop them torching the minister's home. His good humour and nagging sense of guilt had lasted precisely for two days, the time it took for word to reach him that Clay Purnell had not burnt along with the house and church. The buildings had been rendered into ash and Brewes had naturally assumed that Clay Purnell had likewise been rendered into ash.

"Goddamnit," he roared at Parkin. "Can't I trust you to do anything right?" Parkin had been one of the night attackers, the other five being men from neighbouring ranches, and the idea had been their own, thus John Brewes could swear in all honesty that he was not behind the attack on the minister, nor the destruction of church property.

Mrs Brewes had proved to be more concerned with the destruction of the church building than with Clay Purnell's demise and she was now demanding that her husband contribute a substantial sum to the church rebuilding fund.

Feeling himself to be unjustly accused Parkin defended himself. "Hell, boss," he declared, "how could any of us be expected to know that he'd taken himself off to the Red Garter. The last place we'd think he'd go to considering his profession and all. He ain't like no Bible thumper I ever came across before. Why it ain't fitting. Word is he's spending his time shut away with Gracie." He leered at Mrs Brewes who was listening avidly. "Guess we all know what he's getting up to now."

A shocked gasp escaped from Mrs Brewes.

"Bold as you like," Parkin continued. "Don't care who knows about it." A sudden uncomfortable thought occurred to Parkin, "I ain't going after him," he declared. "You ain't paying me gun-fighting wages, boss. If you want Purnell taken out you'll have to pay for the best considering that if he had a mind he'd do very well in that line of work himself."

"We'll have no talk of hired guns," Brewes grunted. Not yet he thought sourly. He knew how to wait. Sometimes waiting paid off, sometimes not and, as yet, he had not figured out what Purnell was liable to do. Hell, if someone had tried to burn him out he'd run them all down and kill every last one of the polecats but Purnell's mind worked in ways plainly impossible to understand. "Get out of my sight Parkin." Brewes knew that Purnell was not a coward and, like Parkin had said, the man was one hell of a fast gun. He'd killed Dan Hater without a qualm, for reasons known only to himself, and if Gracie were to blab that Parkin had been one of the bunch and if Purnell came after Parkin then Parkin was as good as dead.

Days later Brewes had reason to think that waiting had been the right thing to do for Parkin returned from town with the news that Purnell had upped and ridden out with never a word of explanation to anyone. Not even Gracie. And now that Purnell was gone there were those who were saying that he had not deserved to have his house and church burnt out from under him. And the men who'd done the burning were maintaining they'd known all along Clay Purnell was not at home. Finally running out of steam Parkin asked the question uppermost in everyone's mind.

"What the hell are we going to do about those damn woollies?"

Brewes had been wondering about that himself. The woollies were overdue. They should have arrived before now. Something didn't set right and it troubled him. Forgetting about Clay Purnell he gave his thoughts over to more important matters.

"Word is a sheep man brought in

Chivers. He's due to hang once he can walk to the gallows," Parkin continued.
"So that's why the bastard ain't arrived," Brewes observed. He did not think to link Purnell's departure with the outlaw's dire predicament.

* * *

Riding away from Capra Clay did not allow himself to look back. Of necessity he'd been forced to leave and he'd known it wiser not to tell Gracie he was leaving or why. Accordingly he'd snuck out of town feeling damn guilty about it. She deserved better but he remained aware of his pa's words of advice: never trust a woman with a secret, Pa had said, and Clay had been around long enough to know that a truer word had never been spoken.
As the hoofs of his horse ate up the miles to his destination he found himself thinking about Gracie rather than the task which lay ahead of him. Thinking about Gracie was

preferable to acknowledging that he was going to do something which was not exactly right. He had to save Chivers' worthless hide. No way could he not save Chivers' neck from the hangman's noose. Right or wrong he could not let his cousin hang.

And when he'd saved Chivers he was going back for Gracie. And he was finally going to admit that wearing a clerical collar was not for him. He wasn't suited to the work. He'd made one hell of a mistake.

* * *

John Brewes walked into the telegraph office. Solomon, the long streak of misery behind the desk, looked up and smirked. That ought to have to have alerted him that something was wrong.

"Can I help you, Mr Brewes?" Solomon enquired, with another knowing look.

"That's what you're here for ain't

it!" The rancher rested his elbows on the cigarette-burned counter.

"You take your turn, John Brewes," a shrill, feminine voice piped up.

Brewes gaped in astonishment. He'd always been a respected man in this town. He'd ignored the three women because he had other things upon his mind than passing the time of day. Now evidently they'd taken umbrage.

"Take your turn, John Brewes," she repeated. "There'll be no queue-jumping here." She sniffed disapprovingly. He knew then that his status, as seen by these women, had changed. He stared at them in some perplexity wondering what the hell was going on. He didn't know. There was no understanding the female mind.

"It's a wonder," another of them piped up, unabashed by his scowl, "that certain men dare to show their faces in town. What's the world coming to, the church burnt down and our dear minister driven out of town!"

Controlling his temper with difficulty

he endeavoured to set her right. "I had nothing to do with the attack on the Reverend Purnell."

"Your ramrod led the attack."

"What Parkin might or might not do in his free time is not my concern."

"Really, John Brewes, do you take us for fools?"

"Are you calling me a liar?" he bellowed. How the hell had they known about Parkin? How the hell had Purnell known in advance his house was going to be torched? The answer became obvious. The fools had been in the saloon blabbing about their intentions.

Solomon, the telegraph clerk, just about managed to keep a straight face as one of the women retorted, "As we say, John Brewes, we're not fools!" The words were as good as calling Brewes a liar. Had a man uttered them that man would have been knocked flat and doubtless would have felt John Brewes' boots thudding into him.

Confronted with women John Brewes admitted defeat. Contenting himself with a string of epithets he snarled at Solomon, "I'll be back when these" — here he paused, thought better of what he'd been about to say — 'womenfolk,' he concluded lamely, "have been attended to."

He stomped out. Hell, it made no sense. By quitting town Clay Purnell had seemingly won them over. They liked to believe their minister had been run out of town. And instead of naturally concluding the man had a yellow streak down his back he'd become the poor dear minister.

He'd return later. It was his intention to have Solomon wire every town in the vicinity of Capra. He had to know where those stinking woollies were at. He'd have no peace of mind until he discovered their whereabouts.

Spying Gracie marching towards the telegraph office he was tempted to jibe that it had not taken Clay Purnell long to tire of what she had to offer. He thought better of it for she had a bad temper and sharp tongue.

He grinned sourly. Without a doubt Clay Purnell had done one smart thing in his life, a deed for which he could not be faulted, Clay Purnell had had the good sense to get away from Gracie.

Opening the door of the telegraph office with a good deal of unnecessary force Gracie marched in, elbowed a slow and fat townswoman out of her way and glared at Solomon. "A private word if you're agreeable," she snapped.

"Sure Gracie." He was wise enough not to be disagreeable. "Just step on into my private office."

The door of the private office closed behind the two with a resounding slam.

"What was in that telegram you delivered to Clay?" she demanded, without preamble.

"That's private Miss Gracie," he half-heartedly protested.

"You'd better start talking. I'm mad enough to do anything," she warned.

She was certainly crazy enough to do anything he silently corrected. He'd never forgotten that time she'd ridden into town in her underwear. With a shrug of defeat he relayed the message word for word. It hadn't meant a damn thing anyway.

Gracie found herself feeling a trifle more agreeable. He hadn't run out on her as certain folk were supposing. There was a good chance he'd be back. Realization dawned; *if* he didn't get his fool head blown away trying to rescue his good-for-nothing cousin and *if* he wasn't forced to join the owlhoot trail with Chivers.

"Keep your mouth shut!" she warned Solomon.

"Sure," he agreed. The telegram hadn't made a darn bit of sense. It had come from an *hombre* named Ezekiel and had quoted texts from the Good Book.

Out on Main Street Gracie made a snap decision, accordingly instead of swinging right back towards the saloon she swung left and headed for the stage depot.

* * *

Slim Simpson had never experienced such a feeling of euphoria. The reward money had come through pretty damn quick. He was everyone's hero. Folk sought him out to hear him recount the tale of Chivers' apprehension one more time and if the tale changed a mite in the telling no one seemed to notice.

* * *

Slim had taken to maintaining that his foreman, the murdered Manolito, had wanted him to leave Chivers be but knowing his duty he'd refused to entertain the idea. He hadn't thought of the reward at all. He'd gone after Chivers at great risk to himself because it was the right thing to do.

And despite Manolito's warnings, he'd given Chivers and his bunch of cut throats a chance to surrender, what's more Chivers had been waving a white flag when he'd gunned Manolito down.

Yes, there was always plenty to hear the tale, women of the worst kind in particular. He'd been in an upstairs room with two of them last night.

Now, with his head pounding and a sour taste in his mouth, Slim leaned against the batwings of the saloon and eyed the gallows. The carpenters were working hard at it. The noise of the falling hammers reverberated in his head, the thudding causing real pain. Damnit, how much had he drunk last night? He vaguely recalled that there had been a bottle or two of best brandy. And those girls had amazed him by swallowing down the fiery liquid without so much as a cough.

He became aware of a further discomfort. An itching beneath his arms. He scratched vigorously. Being a sheep man he had an idea of his complaint. He needed to get over to the bathhouse, get himself a hot tub and then afterwards apply a generous application of lice salve.

He took an uncertain step! The world spun. The buildings appeared to move. Slim fell flat upon his face.

"Want a hand, Mr Simpson?"

Slim grinned foolishly. It was Mr Simpson now, not that damn sheep herder. "I sure do, son. Just as far as the bathhouse. And if you care to join me at the saloon I'll be glad to show my appreciation."

"Sure thing, Mr Simpson." The youth guided Slim towards the bathhouse. He'd been counting on an invite.

* * *

Clay had ridden long and hard pushing his horse as much as was reasonably possible without running the animal into the ground. He'd been forced to it for he had no way of knowing just when the necktie party was scheduled to take place. It had been his great fear that he would not arrive until after the event.

Therefore the sight of the gallows going up occasioned a feeling of pleasure. He was in time.

Had it not been near enough exhausted, his horse would have unseated him. As it was it did not have the energy to rear up as a parcel of over excited young ones crossed Clay's path, turning cartwheels and whooping with glee. Clay frowned. He knew damn well why the kids were over excited. They were looking forward to the sight of a man dancing at the end of a rope. Even decent, honest, hard-working folk did not think to keep their young ones away from such an event. He cursed softly.

Dismounting, he sniffed the air and smelt roast lamb. Eyeing the eating-house directly opposite the scaffold he noted a sign in the window proclaiming *Roast lamb courtesy of Mr Slim Simpson*. From behind the eating-house came the bleating of woollies; a quick look showed him six of the animals penned up waiting their turn for roasting.

His legs ached. Town living unfortunately made a man soft. Why, a while back, a ride like the one he'd undertaken would not have troubled him none. Now he was paying the price.

How the hell was he going to save Chivers? He'd expected the answer to come to him along the trail. A forlorn hope. It had not.

Stiffly he headed for the livery barn.

"Stay around," the ostler advised. "Town's putting on a show."

"When's the hanging?" Clay asked, wondering how much time he had to come up with an answer.

"Straight after the trial," the ostler responded.

"He ain't been tried!" Clay exclaimed.

"Nope. Judge took the fever on his way here. We had to postpone Chivers' day of reckoning. But it'll be coming soon. Doc says he's on the mend."

Clay nodded. "How soon?"

"Can't say," the ostler rejoined.

"I'm obliged." Clay moved away from the livery barn reflecting grimly that leastways he had time for a long, hot soak in the tub and after that he'd have a meal of roast lamb, the smell of it having wetted his appetite. Maybe the answer to his problem would come to him whilst he lay in the tub.

* * *

Slim Simpson lay back. He rested his head upon the rim of the tub. The water lapping around his bony legs was black with filth. He eyed the pot of salve. Rub in well he'd been advised. Slim knew the ointment would feel like he was being burned.

"Worth its weight in gold," the owner of the bathhouse, a dour Scotsman, had exclaimed. Slim didn't know why the man had to look so damn miserable for he was charging enough for the ointment. It might just as well have been gold.

Desperate men didn't argue Slim

thought, watching two small Chinese workers hauling large and heavy pails in for the filling of another tub. His mind registered the fact they were performing this task without spilling a drop.

Clouds of steam filled the room. Slim shut his eyes. He just might, on his way out, if he spotted a full pail, kick that damn pail over!

Sitting up, Slim opened his eyes and saw Chivers!

Fear hit his guts. He couldn't think straight. The bastard was out and had come to get the man who'd killed his men, hauled him in for the rope. His senses were not so dulled that he did not know what to do. He did what any man intent on self-preservation would do, lunged for the .45 lying on the stool beside his tub.

A troubled and tired man, Clay Purnell's reaction to danger was not as sharp as it ought to have been. He was taken completely unaware. He saw the man, a lanky beanpole of a man he'd never seen in his life, lunging for the

.45, water spraying all around puddling the floor. Too late Clay realized the danger. A complete stranger aimed to kill him.

He was done for. His mind registered that fact as his hand desperately reached for his own .45. As he drew the gun he felt pain as he'd never felt before. In the region of his side. He'd been hit. Desperately he levelled his weapon, it felt to heavy for his hand, he could scarcely move his arm upwards but he knew he must make the attempt whilst he still had a chance of saving himself.

Slim's hand had been shaking so much that his slug had failed to kill. A dark stain was spreading over the man's dust-covered shirt, the man clutched at his side with one hand as with the other he attempted to line up on Slim.

The man was not Chivers . . . the knowledge temporarily froze Slim, pretty close but not the bank robber.

"I never . . . "

It was too late, for the stranger's

bullet struck him fair and square in the chest. He crumpled forward to hang over, way over the tub, his blood turning the water a rusty red.

Dimly, Clay's mind registered the fact that there'd been no second bullet. And then everything plunged into total blackness, a blackness unbroken except for a shining shimmering light, like the light thrown out by a firefly or a soul leaving a body for the ultimate journey Clay thought, as he fell to the floor.

* * *

Ezekiel Chivers opened his eyes. The door which separated the cells from the main office was shut and bolted, but not thick enough to keep out the sound of raised voices. He pricked up his ears. He could not quite make out what was being said. Something about the bathhouse and that damn sheep man. He strained his ears but failed to pick up further information. Silence fell. Presumably the sheriff was on his way to the bathhouse.

Absentmindedly he scratched his legs. The cell was infested with fat, brown, blood-sucking bugs. They crawled out from the crevices at night whilst he slept and had themselves a good feed. Damn it if they'd give him a light and a candle he'd show them bugs a thing or two.

But bugs he admitted were the least of his problems. His stomach growled with hunger. The sheriff, once again, purposely had forgotten to feed him.

It was not until late afternoon when the kid who earned a few dollars cleaning up and running errands for the fat fool of a sheriff came in with a hunk of stale bread and mug of water that Ezekiel learned the truth. He'd hang after all.

Clay had not let him down. Despite his odd way of thinking these days, Clay had come through but Clay lay seriously wounded, blasted by that damn crazy sheep man.

The boy, who admired, secretly, the

bank robber, took pleasure in relating how the sheep man had gone crazy, tried to kill a minister, except the Reverend Clay Purnell had not looked much like a minister. Clay Purnell was in a bad way so Doc said.

"Thanks kid," Chivers dismissed the youngster. He regretted having sent for Clay. Guilt assailed him. Why he'd even thought Clay might have ignored the plea for help. But Clay whatever he was these days was still Clay.

Chivers chomped at his bread. The bugs had better make the best of it. His time with them wouldn't be overlong. Leastways Slim Simpson had been denied the chance of watching a better man dance at the end of a rope. Chivers took grim satisfaction from it. And from the fact the reward money had not done the sheep man any damn good. The undertaker would pocket it now. Unless they'd gone through his clothes at the bathhouse.

Giving up hope he resigned himself to the inevitable, it not being until a few days later that he was able to take any kind of interest in what was going on in the outer office. It was the sound of a woman's voice which succeeded in bringing him out of the lethargy which, quite naturally, had assailed him once he'd accepted there was no way now that he could cheat the hangman's noose.

Whoever she was she was riling Trump for he heard the sheriff roar at her to get the hell out of it.

"Very well. I'll be back. Don't you imagine that you've heard the last of this."

The connecting door swung open. Chivers smelt the roast lamb. He understood that everyone in town was eating roast lamb, free of charge, courtesy of the lately departed Slim Simpson. Except himself of course. Trump was more or less trying to starve him during his last remaining days. Not that there were any remaining days left. Tomorrow he would hang.

Leastways it looked as though Clay

had pulled through. The deputy had volunteered that snippet of information. Chivers had known better than to ask, not wanting anyone to make a connection between the two of them.

Trump appeared in the doorway chewing on a leg of roast lamb and advising, "You won't need a full belly where you're going."

"You've said your piece so just shut the damn door. The sight of your ugly face is enough to turn a man's stomach," Chivers retorted, knowing that Trump had more to say. And he'd guessed right.

"Looks like your wife has run you down. She's set on seeing you!" Trump guffawed. "But like I told her she must get through me and I ain't stepping aside."

It was with great difficulty Chivers kept his expression impassive. There was no Mrs Chivers. Trump was a fool. "I've advised her if she wants to see you to present herself outside the jail tomorrow afternoon, after folk have had their midday siesta. That's when you're set to hang."

Chivers shrugged. "You've said your piece. Now get." He was intrigued. Mrs Chivers indeed. And now she was back. He could hear her in the outer office calling out loudly for the sheriff.

Trump swung around, "I thought I told you to get the hell out of it."

"I want to speak to you, Sheriff Trump." Chivers recognized the voice of the minister. The man, together with his Good Book, had presented himself at the jail sometime earlier and Chivers had decidedly told Minister Davison to go to hell.

"What in tarnation!" Trump grumbled, clearly puzzled by this new development.

Through the partly open door he listened to the argument which now ensued, a grin spreading over his face. Trump had been out-smarted by the woman calling herself Mrs Chivers.

Davison's voice rose with righteous fury. "You'll not hear the end of this. I'll denounce you from the pulpit if you keep the Lord's word from a condemned man."

"I'll have to search her," Trump conceded defeat. Chivers could imagine the leer upon the sheriff's face.

"Indeed you will not, Sheriff Trump," Davison snapped. "Mrs Davison had already searched Mrs Chivers. Do you take me for a fool!"

The woman spoke up now. "I'm a respectable woman for all I made the mistake of marrying a man inclined to wrong-doing. But I know my duty. He will have the family Bible to comfort him during his last night."

"That's all he will have," Trump retorted angrily, clearly put out at not being able to get his hands upon Mrs Chivers. "I'll have no hanky-panky in my cells."

There then followed the sound of a resounding slap.

"Why you . . ."

"Sheriff Trump!" Davison's voice rose warningly. "You deserved that, Trump. Well done, Mrs Chivers."

"Hell, get in there then and give him the Bible but don't be long about it," Trump blustered.

The woman wasn't what he'd been expecting. She wore a faded gingham dress, apron and huge bonnet which went a long way towards obscuring her face. He then caught a glimpse of a side-buttoned boot and black silk stocking! Carefully she closed the connecting door, and turned to him. Her voice of necessity low.

"Now listen carefully you good-for-nothing polecat." She waved the large black Book before the bars but kept it just out of his reach. "Before you get this Book you must agree to one condition." She paused and concluded despairingly, "Your fool of a cousin maintains you ain't a liar."

"That I'm not!" He was desperate to get his hands upon what he knew to be a hollowed-out Bible and its content a most useful snub-nosed derringer. “What condition is Clay setting?” Haggling wasn’t Clay’s way!

“None,” she declared. “I’m setting the condition. You’ll get this Bible when you swear you’ll take passage out, passage to anywhere at all, Europe, Australia, and you’ll never come back, not ever.” She actually smiled. “Always assuming you don’t get shot to pieces whilst attempting to escape from this flea-bitten hole. I came up with the idea of getting you out of here so I’m setting the terms. Clay isn’t taken with the idea of me risking my neck on account of you.”

“Why?”

She shrugged. “Clay had it in his mind to attempt getting you out tonight despite the fact that he ain’t fit to walk let alone ride a horse.”

“Why the condition?” He was a puzzled man. He could understand her concern on Clay’s behalf but not the terms.

She winked. "Why, I aim to marry Clay Purnell and I'm damned if I want you around unsettling my married life. What's your answer. Yes or no?"

He shrugged. "Naturally, ma'am, I agree to your condition and the Lord help Cousin Clay that's all I've got to say. Know about your intentions does he?"

She smiled. "That's none of your concern, Chivers. Take the Book and good luck to you. And goodbye. I don't ever want to see you again." She pulled out a large white handkerchief. "You're damn lucky Ezekiel Chivers. Damn lucky I arrived here in time to save your worthless hide."

"Yes, ma'am," he agreed readily, his spirits lifting for he stood a chance after all.

"It ain't every day a woman's husband gets hung. I'm taking the stage out this afternoon in order to miss the distressing sight." She began to sob as she hammered upon the connecting door.

Chivers grinned. Too bad, he reflected, that he would not be afforded a chance to warn Clay that the woman meant to hog-tie him. Too bad Clay wasn't up and able to run.

7

RUNNING down Main Street Solomon, the telegraph clerk, tripped and stumbled, going down upon his hands and knees in the dust. A farm buggy had to swerve violently to avoid running over him and the driver delivered a string of loud curses together with an observation about fools. Righting himself Solomon sprinted towards the Red Garter, bursting through the batwings as though a tornado were behind him.

"He's dead!"

"Who?" John Brewes turned away from the bar thinking it was too much to expect that the words referred to Clay Purnell. The Devil, as they said, looked after his own. Everyone in town was still blaming him for the minister's abrupt departure and the destruction of the church. Mrs Brewes had been asked to leave the sewing circle!

"Why that damn sheep man. Who else!" Solomon declared, amazed that his words had been received mostly without interest.

"You don't say!" He had the rancher's attention now.

"I do say," Solomon declared, filled with self-importance. He gulped. "Shot dead by Clay Purnell himself. Brought it upon himself he did. Word is the sheep man tried to blast the reverend as he was fixing to take himself a bath. Reverend didn't have no choice but to blast him."

"Now why would anyone want to kill Clay Purnell?" Brewes asked his expression sour.

"Don't make no sense." The speaker took the question at face value. Brewes' scowl deepened.

"And Chivers has escaped the noose," Solomon continued, as though this information was a mere afterthought. "Broke out of jail the night before they were due to stretch his neck. Shot the sheriff in the leg and all." He scratched his head. "I wonder why he didn't finish him off? Must be getting soft."

"What else?" Brewes enquired.

"Trump denies all responsibility for the escape. If they've figured out how Chivers got hold of a weapon they ain't letting on."

Brewes downed his whiskey. "Wouldn't be surprised if Clay Purnell hadn't a hand in this."

Solomon shook his head vigorously. "That ain't so. Clay's been shot up bad, hardly able to walk across the room let alone get himself to the jail."

So it was Clay now was it. He knew the polecat would be back. To a hero's welcome for he had killed the sheep man. That one deed had dramatically changed the esteem in which folk held Purnell. Next thing they'd be saying Purnell had saved the town from out-and-out war.

A sobering thought struck Brewes.

Simpson's land was darn good land and with the sheep man dead the land would be up for grabs. Unfortunately Brewes did not at this time have capital to spare, his wealth was vast but most of it was tied up in land and cattle. If the bidding went high he wouldn't have the cash. He'd best then have Parkin spread the word to any local interested parties that John Brewes had his eye on that land.

John Brewes failed to appreciate that another outsider might come in.

★ ★ ★

"You ain't crossing my land!" The dirtbuster's voice and stance was defiant. Feet planted apart he was resolved to stand firm; rifle cradled under his arm he stood ready to raise it at any moment despite the fact that he was vastly outgunned. "You cowmen think you own the range, well, you don't. You ain't got no more rights than the rest of us." And then as the cattleman made no response he continued recklesly, "I filed claim to this land six months past. It's mine and I say who passes over. That's a fact. Better stick it in your pipe."

Bert Magnalia nodded. "I'll do that friend." His voice was deceptively mild. Magnalia never allowed his rage to show for it gave folk fair warning that trouble was coming. He reckoned it was always best to take folk by surprise. Contenting himself therefore with that brief response he wheeled his horse and rode back towards his herd his ramrod riding just a mite behind.

Reining his horse Magnalia surveyed his cattle, strung out and thirsty. Water lay beyond the farmer's miserable patch of dirt.

"Make him an offer, boss. He'll reconsider. Land won't be giving him much of a living and he'll have a brood of young ones with empty bellies."

"No," Magnalia spoke decisively. "Firstly the man's as obstinate as a mule. And secondly there's no cause to negotiate. I'm a man in a position of strength."

"Sure, boss," the ramrod agreed, thinking that Bert Magnalia had the coldest blue eyes he had come across, peculiar eyes for they kind of squinted. Malevolently if you cared to think about it.

"I'm a business man," Magnalia stated with a trace of pride. Justifiable pride he considered for none of his varied ventures had failed to make a considerable profit. Now he was foraying in the world of ranching, temporarily, for Magnalia had no love for the land and the wide-open spaces old cowpokes waxed lyrical about. It was his intention to make a quick buck and then pull out, not that any of the simpletons he had hired were aware of his true intentions. He rubbed his chin. "I can understand why ranching men can't abide uppity dirt-farmers."

"It'll take longer going round," the ramrod mused.

"When you get to know me better

you'll know I never waste time. I can't abide time-wasters. Time is money. You've heard that saying ain't you? Well, it's true." He shrugged. "I've wasted enough time on that fool dirtbuster, now here's what I want doing." Succinctly he explained how they were to proceed. "That's what we've got to do," he concluded. "Ignore all obstacles between us and our destination. Have you any queries? Do you understand?"

"Sure, boss." Stirwell shrugged. "You've spelt it out plain. Like you've said he's brung it upon himself."

Having outfaced the cattleman, the dirtbuster retreated to his dugout. Inside the dugout he was king ruling over his faded wife and eight scrawny children.

"Well I told him good," he declared. "Said I would and I did."

"You sure did Pa," an undernourished boy piped up.

"He could see I meant business."

His wife continued to rock the baby.

"They could see damn well that I was prepared to make a fight of it."

She rocked harder. Her husband was a fool. How many cowpokes were out there nursing the herd along, twenty, maybe more and he'd told them that he was ready to make a fight of it. She'd been prepared to hear the sound of gun shots any moment.

Stirwell relayed the boss's instructions. "The boss ain't asking you personally to hurt a hair on that dirtbuster's head. You're to leave him be. If the man can get himself out of the dugout that's his good luck, if he can't that's his bad luck. Whatever happens it ain't none of our concern. Now, get them bunched afore we allow them to make a run for the water. Boss wants them running in a straight line." The fact that the straight line led through the cornfield and over the dugout was not referred to. "I've advised the boss that we'll maybe lose a few but he reckons that can't be avoided. He's allowed for wastage." In other words time would not be wasted whilst the men scoured the surrounds for strays.

Inside the dugout they heard the shot and the whooping and then the thunder of hoofs. Realization dawned. The woman screamed. The man snatched up his rifle. And ran outside to see death thundering towards him. He fired just the one shot before he went down beneath the hoofs. The noise of the cattle drowned the screams from inside the dugout and the swirling choking red dust hid the miserable hovel from view. When the dust cleared the dugout was practically undetectable for it had been flattened. None of the men responsible paused to wonder just how many might have been inside the dugout.

Bert Magnalia observed that certain of his hands appeared to be getting a great deal of satisfaction from the fact that their cattle had flattened the dugout. Magnalia himself felt nothing at all. The man, as he had said, had just been an obstacle to be ruthlessly removed.

Dismissing the dirtbuster from his mind his thoughts turned towards other matters. There could be obstacles waiting for him in Capra.

John Brewes now, the town's biggest rancher, well, the man would surely be bearing a grudge for Brewes had bid for the land. Magnalia's agent had dutifully reported back that Brewes had looked fit to burst with rage when he had been outbid.

And then there was the sheriff, Gaskill, a man advancing in years but still a lethal killer, a man without principle who could be bought by the highest bidder. Gaskill could not be trusted for Magnalia believed the man to be capable of taking retainers both from himself and John Brewes. Brewes was a man after his own heart: Brewes wouldn't balk at murder. Word was that Brewes in a fit of rage had tried to have the town's minister burned to death one night.

And failed. That was a good omen. When Bert Magnalia set his mind to doing something he did not fail. John Brewes had failed. The minister was still around. Twice men had tried to kill him, first John Brewes and then the sheep man Simpson. Both times the man had escaped. Word was Dan Hater had died in Capra but Magnalia did not know how that had come about. Enquiries into Hater's death had met with a wall of silence. As Magnalia knew small towns could be closed-mouth places when they had a mind.

It was Parkin's lot to bring word to Brewes that the new outfit had arrived and moved on to what had been Twisted M Range. Moreover the new owner an *hombre* answering to the handle of Magnalia was reviving the old brand. Also, in Parkin's opinion, Magnalia must be a greenhorn when it came to ranching for quite clearly the man was over stocking his range.

Moreover Magnalia was stringing wire around Lizard Head creek for all that only part of the creek was on his land. Magnalia was taking it all.

That information brought Brewes to his feet cursing loudly. Not that Brewes used the creek himself but the neighbour, a man Brewes contemptuously referred to as Two Bits, a man whose land acted as a buffer between Brewes and Twisted M range, in time of drought Two Bits relied heavily upon Lizard Head Creek to get him through trying times.

Various notions, all of them unpleasant, presented themselves to John Brewes. Over stocked the Twisted M cattle would need additional grazing space. What better than Two Bits' spread? Moreover the boundary between Brewes' land and Two Bits' land was not clearly defined a fact which hitherto had not bothered him for Two Bits presented no threat.

Magnalia was an entirely different matter.

Brewes found himself recalling the pike which had lurked in a murky pool near to Brewes' home town. Many a time had the young John Brewes tried to land that pike without success; it had just lurked in deep water only moving to gobble up the smaller fish. Magnalia put him in mind of that pike. A big fish surrounded by small fish. Brewes felt a surge of fury. Next thing Magnalia would be trying to ingratiate himself with the Cattlemen's Association.

Parkin retreated. "If you want to make his acquaintance, boss, he's in town. Gone in for supplies and to make himself known to the Association."

Parkin exited his boss's office in the nick of time, a heavy brass ashtray thudding against the closing door.

* * *

Magnalia took Stirwell and some of his men into town with him. He believed first impressions were important and knew damn well he'd make more of an impression if he rode in with his hard-bitten crew rather than ride in solo.

Leaving his order with the storekeeper he led his men into the nearest saloon and magnanimously bought each a beer and a cigar.

Shrugging off the hand of an overpainted woman who did her best to detain him, he strode through the batwings out on the Main Street. He was no fool; why pay for it when he could indulge for nothing? Well, practically nothing; the Mexican girl he'd picked up along the trail had cost him two sacks of flour and one steer.

Locating the hotel which housed the office of the Cattlemen's Association, Magnalia made his way there. True, the girl spent her time crying and there wasn't much life in her but she wasn't costing and that was the main thing. Magnalia had always possessed a healthy respect for money. It went against the grain to waste his money on a woman.

From inside her eating-house Dora watched the bare-footed girl climb out of the wagon situated in front of the general store. The girl didn't look too happy. Not being entirely without compassion Dora sauntered over. "Can I help you?"

The girl flinched as though she had been struck and mumbled something about the sheriff.

"Gaskill!" Dora snorted contemptuously. "He won't help you if you need to get away. And I reckon you do. It's the minister you'll be needing. You'll find him over at the Red Garter. Thank the Lord that dressed-up little jackass ain't patronizing the Red Garter today. It's safe enough for you to go in. Go on now. Reverend Purnell knows what's right and what ain't. Oh, come on girl. I'll take you to him myself." Dora could see the unfortunate girl was too afraid to go into the saloon. Taking hold of the girl's hand Dora dragged her through the batwings of the Red Garter.

There wasn't much going on inside the place, just a few men loafing against the bar. One or two tired-looking girls who looked as though they had gotten out of bed just a while ago and Gracie.

Gracie threw Dora a mocking smile. "If you're hoping to be shocked, Dora, it's the wrong time. Come back night-time," she drawled.

"Huh," Dora snorted. "It would take a good deal more than what goes on in here to shock me, Gracie. Is Clay around? This girl needs help!"

"She ain't connected with the outfit which has just ridden in is she?" Gracie enquired.

"She sure is."

"Then take her to the sheriff. I don't want to see Clay involving himself in gunplay."

"I would if we had ourselves a decent lawman. But Gaskill ain't a decent lawman. We both know that. Now, will you get Clay or must I go up and get him myself?"

"Hell, I'll get him then," Gracie rejoined. She scowled at Dora. "And if he gets blasted I'll hold you personally responsible."

"Well he ain't likely to get blasted," Dora responded, untroubled by the implied threat. "We all know that Clay now, well, he ain't exactly suited to preaching. Gunslinging is what he's darn good at. This girl needs help and if he don't help her then no one will."

"Oh he'll help her sure enough," Gracie rejoined grimly, as she set off up stairs to fetch Clay. Privately she determined to work on Clay. The sooner they could shake the dust of this darn town off their boots the better for both of them.

* * *

Stretching out his legs Magnalia gave a satisfied grunt. He'd been accepted. Made welcome. His armchair was comfortable and the brandy the best he had ever tasted. There was nothing he liked better than playing the gentleman.

He smiled complacently but the smile faded when Stirwell having brushed aside the objections of the desk clerk burst unceremoniously into the room.

"That bitch," he shouted, "she was in the wagon all along and now she's sneaked into the Red Garter saloon."

"Lower your voice, man," Magnalia snapped, face darkening. A sudden silence had fallen and everyone was watching and listening.

"They ain't booted her out. She's still inside." Stirwell lowered his voice but as no one else was talking it made no difference.

"Get her out."

"Suppose she don't want to come."

"Get her out I said."

"Hold on there ramrod," a weather-lined rancher spoke up. "Don't you go barging into the Red Garter looking for trouble, do you hear?" He paused significantly. "The minister is in there."

"What!" Magnalia rounded on the speaker. And then he laughed. "Don't tell me the minister is a damn drunk."

"I ain't telling you that," the speaker continued, face grave. "He lives there you see." There was a pause. "On account of his church and house being burnt down."

Magnalia spluttered with disgust. "Hell, what kind of minister has this town got?" He dismissed the minister as being of no account. "Just get that girl, Stirwell. Take a couple of the men with you."

"Sure, boss."

"He won't back down, not Clay Purnell," the rancher continued. "And he'll use his gun if need be." By now he was speaking to an empty space, Stirwell having departed. He rose to his feet. "Guess I'll mosey over to the Red Garter and watch what transpires. Ought to be interesting. I'm betting on Purnell. Any takers?"

To Magnalia's disbelief the room proceeded to empty. Momentarily he was a forgotten man. Someone of no importance.

* * *

Clay scowled. "Darn it, Gracie, will you get inside?" he said, for the umpteenth time. "And you, too, Dora." Both women were upstairs on the balcony which overlooked the saloon floor. The young girl was inside Gracie's room sobbing.

"I'm holding you personally responsible for my mirrors!" the weasel who owned the Red Garter said again. "If you make it, Minister, I'll expect you to reimburse me for breakages."

"There'll be something else broken beside your mirrors," Clay snapped. "Back off before I forget I don't hold with violence!" Even as he spoke five hardcases came through the batwings. Just one look at them told him that whether he held with violence or not he was going to have to resort to it. Words would be wasted upon these men.

Suddenly unsure of himself Stirwell studied the minister. The man was not what he had expected to find.

He had expected to find a maudlin drunk sitting at a table or propping up the bar. A nobody to be pushed aside. This man was no drunk and he had, in Stirwell's opinion, the eyes of a gunfighter. Cold eyes. Eyes which weren't afraid. You could tell much from a man's eyes, Stirwell had discovered. Most men would have been afraid but not this one.

Clay Purnell, Minister of Capra, was well over six foot. He was a large man with broad shoulders and powerful-looking arms. He was all muscle. In keeping with his profession he wore a dark suit and white shirt topped by the obligatory stiff collar. Blond hair just reached the shoulders of his suit.

Significantly the minister also wore a Colt .45 strapped low at the hip. He looked comfortable with his gun, the holster, not new and bright but well worn, conveying the impression Clay Purnell and his .45 had been together a mighty long time.

"Good day," the Minister spoke up. Voice pleasant enough but eyes as cold as ice. He did not smile.

Stirwell cleared his throat. "We've come for the girl." The words came out as a croak. "The boss wants her back. He ain't ready to let her go yet awhile."

"I thought slavery had been abolished."

"You tell your boss to go to hell," a grey-haired, gimlet-eyed woman up on the balcony shrilled. "That girl don't want no more to do with him. This is a decent town. We don't countenance such goings-on here."

The ramrod was undecided. The eyes betrayed the man's indecision.

"You try and take the girl and there'll be death in here," Clay warned softly.

"Yours, Preacher."

The shifty-eyed hardcase standing alongside the ramrod reached for his iron. Clay had seen it coming. And he'd anticipated the move. His own hand swept down, the heavy cumbersome Colt slid out of its,holster and Clay fired.

"Don't shoot, Minister. We ain't reaching." The word emerged as a thin screech. The other four stood as if rooted.

"You damn fools," Clay snarled, his smoking gun covering them. "When a man pulls iron his every instinct is to blast everyone in sight. That's protective instinct. You don't know how close you came."

* * *

Although it had humbled him to do so Magnalia found himself following in the wake of the others. Even before they reached the saloon there was the sound of a shot.

"Hell, Purnell's gone and blasted one of them before we got there."

"Fun's over. Here comes Gaskill."

Magnalia turned. The man hurrying towards the saloon was a small man. A man who wore a pin-striped suit and put the cattleman in mind of a travelling salesman.

"A word of warning, Mr Magnalia. Don't cross Gaskill. Hell, the polecat works on his bullets. Cuts them so they splinter when they go into a man. So I've heard tell."

Someone sniggered. "You'll be in hot water, Mr Magnalia, if Clay Purnell is lying dead in there. Gaskill's wife is a staunch member of the minister's congregation. That's why he's here. She's sent him to save Clay's hide."

Magnalia's eyes narrowed. Men were moving out of Gaskill's way without having to be asked. The sheriff looked furious. "I'll get round to you later," he all but snarled at the cattleman.

"Well, Sheriff, you took your time getting here," Dora shrilled, as the lawman burst into the saloon.

"That ain't surprising as no one thought fit to inform me what was going on," Gaskill rejoined.

"How'd you know?" she asked curiously. "I guess Mrs Gaskill found out from the storekeep. And as for not informing you there's a damn good reason for that. This town had gotten the kind of law-man it deserves."

Gaskill fumed silently. No man would have dared to say that to him. He rounded on the four hardcases. "Get that trash out of here." He jerked his head towards the dead man. "You step out of line again and I'll blast you myself. Understand?"

"There's been a misunderstanding Sheriff." Magnalia came into the saloon oily features composed into a grin of sorts. "Naturally the female in question is free to do whatever she chooses."

"She's going to work in my restaurant. And if she goes missing we'll know where to look." Dora glared at the cattleman. She'd never cottoned to men who plastered their hair down with grease. Nor wore suits a mite too tight. Not to mention starched shirts. And the man's eyes were most peculiar. They kind of squinted.

"I wouldn't take it kindly if that

girl were to disappear out of Dora's restaurant," Gaskill said. Personally he didn't give a damn but if Clay Purnell were to get himself killed on account of this his wife would give him hell.

Biting back his rage Magnalia tried to retrieve the situation. It was imperative to win Gaskill over. He eyed Stirwell, hiding his annoyance with the man's inefficiency. Stirwell could follow orders but he'd never be able to improvise and that was what it was all about.

"I have no further use for the girl. I don't give a damn what she does." Ignoring the preacher he turned towards the sheriff. "May I buy you a brandy, Sheriff? Over at the Association?"

Gaskill shrugged. "Why not. We ought to understand each other, Mr Magnalia." He winked at Clay. "Be seeing you around, Purnell. Try your darnest not to blast anyone will you? You're here to save souls, ain't you? Not to despatch them to the hereafter." He actually grinned at his own joke.

Having been thus dismissed Clay holstered his gun. The smell of gunsmoke hung in the air. He became aware of Gracie at his side.

"You're lucky to be alive. Five to one ain't good odds. Clay!" She took his arm. "Let's leave this damn town. Why don't we get married and start over some place else. Some decent place where we ain't known."

She'd said the last thing he'd expected her to say and Clay felt as though he had been socked hard upon the jaw. If he'd been thinking straight he would have thought before speaking. As it was he heard himself say, "I ain't ready, Gracie. That's a mighty important step you're talking about. I ain't sure."

"You ain't sure!" she frowned. "You were sure enough up in my room." Her voice rose. Too late, Clay noted tears well up in her eyes. She blinked furiously. "You ain't sure. I ain't good enough for you. That's it." She picked up a whiskey bottle. "Get. Get the hell out of my saloon and my room. Get out now or I won't be responsible."

Aware that he'd put his foot in it Clay backed slowly towards the batwings. Careless words had hurt her. And made her furious. As he exited through the batwings the whiskey bottle she'd been holding splintered against the wall an inch or so away from the back of his head.

Even as he stood upon the sidewalk outside the Red Garter his few belongings came hurtling out of the window. He felt his face begin to grow red. Folk were sniggering. It wasn't the show they'd expected to see but it was good enough.

"You've shamed that woman," Dora hissed. She'd followed him out. "Turned her down publicly. She won't forget it. Not Gracie." She sniffed. "Still it had to end some time, you being a minister and all."

8

JESS WHITE, commonly known as Two Bits, was a worried man. Jess had been worrying about something or other most of his life but now he really had cause for concern. A man didn't need to be particularly bright to know that the newcomer Magnalia was trying to squeeze him out.

The moot point was Lizard Head Creek. Lizard Head Creek lay part on Jess's range and part on the range belonging to the new man. The exact boundaries had never been clearly defined. And now Magnalia had infringed upon land that had always been deemed to belong to Jess White. And strung barbed wire, effectively stopping Jess from getting at water which he had always considered belonged to him.

An indecisive man Jess didn't know

what to do. Except wait. Wait and hope John Brewes would take action. Not that Brewes cared a damn about his neighbour Jess White, Jess wasn't fool enough to believe that. But Magnalia's intention was plain enough; if Magnalia succeeded in taking over White land then, like as not, Magnalia would turn his attention to range belonging to John Brewes. Jess's spread was between the two of them, Brewes and Magnalia. And to be fair to Brewes he had never tried to appropriate land that was not his to take.

The gall of Magnalia was unbelievable. Already Magnalia's beef was drifting on to White land.

Jess hoped and prayed Brewes would do something. That something being to kill Magnalia. Brewes knew what was at stake. He'd sent word to Jess, if needs be Jess could drive his cattle on to Brewes' own range and avail himself of the water thereon. John Brewes must be playing a waiting game, waiting for the right moment to strike, trying to keep his neighbour from going under.

Jess chewed his lower lip. He didn't know how long he could hang on, it being a hell of a trek to the water Brewes had made available. And Gaskill was keeping out of it. Word was Magnalia had bought his co-operation. Not that anyone could trust Gaskill or know what he might do. Now if Purnell was the sheriff of Capra things would be a mite different.

Clementine White, who was pegging out the weekly wash, bit back the words she wanted to say. Jess didn't know what to do. To Clementine it was obvious what they had to do. She wasn't packing up a wagon and moving on. Life was hard enough here. Elsewhere it would be worse. Why couldn't Jess see what had to be done she asked herself yet again. She saw the riders heading towards their ranch house before he did.

"Riders coming in, Jess!"

"Best get inside the house, Mother," he advised. "Bolt the door and keep the rifle handy. Whatever happens out in the yard don't you come out now."

His wife wasn't listening. Already she was racing to round up the various young ones. Two of them started bawling, not wanting to go inside. Jess heard a resounding slap then the thud of the door.

And even before Magnalia's men had got to him he was starting to perspire. He wiped his damp hands on the worn seat of his pants and prayed the fear he felt would not show in his eyes. His youngsters were watching and Jess didn't want their last memory of their father to be of a coward. He was under no illusions. Anything might happen. Magnalia could have sent them with orders to blast him on some pretext or other.

There were four horses Jess saw. Bile rose in his stomach. But only three riders. The fourth horse carried a body. And Jess knew who it was. His hired hand. An honest, hard-working oldster presumably butchered by the polecats who worked for Magnalia. And he knew why they'd brought the murdered man home personally. They aimed to provoke him into making a foolish move. Then they'd gun him down. A single tear rolled down his weather-lined cheek, he rated old Mat highly.

And, Good Lord, how he wanted to bring his rifle up and blast those grinning killers out of the saddle. He wanted it more than anything. And that was what they were waiting for. Hoping for. He stayed motionless. Rooted to the spot. Knowing he'd already failed old Mat. Mat would not have hesitated to blast away. Mat had been a better man than Jess White could ever be.

The one called Stirwell cut the ropes which bound the body. With a thud old Mat hit dirt. Stirwell grinned showing tobacco-stained teeth. "Couldn't be helped, Jess," he said apologetically. "We caught him at the wire. Yelled at him to stop cutting but the old fool hauled iron. We had no choice but to blast him. He'd been given fair warning sure enough." He let the words hang in the air waiting for a reaction.

A muscle of Jess's right cheek twitched. He forgot his earlier resolution to stoically take whatever they ditched out. "You damn liar. Mat wasn't carrying no cutters and he was nowhere near that damned wire," he growled.

Stirwell's grin broadened. The fool of a rancher had fallen right into the trap. Deliberately he struck Jess White across the mouth cutting White's lip and drawing blood. "No man calls me a liar. Either you get down and lick my boots by way of apology or you get ready to reach for your iron."

"Better get licking if you want to keep living, Two Bits," Stirwell's sidekick jeered. The other man guffawed.

Jess White knew he was going to die. He could not, would not eat crow. Even if he'd done what Stirwell had demanded they would kill him anyway. That was why they were here. All he could do now was to die bravely.

"I'm ready when you are," he replied calmly.

"You men keep out of this. I'll handle this solo," Stirwell advised his men. "Easiest job I've ever done," he boasted. White was a hard-working rancher. No gunman. Easy meat. He swung down from the saddle and the two men faced each other both ready. But Stirwell didn't reach. Not yet. He prolonged the moment. He wanted to see White break. The best part of it was always when they begged for mercy.

"Move, damn it. Move!" Clementine White bit her lip until it started to bleed. "Move, Jess. Move, you fool."

Unaware of course that his wife intended taking a hand Jess White, with agonizing slowness, did indeed begin to move.

"Thank the Lord," Clementine heaved a sigh of relief. Her husband having moved himself out of her line of fire had left her with a clear shot at Stirwell and his two pards. Clementine sighted her pa's old Sharps buffalo gun. It was heavy and packed a hell of a punch. She sighted on Stirwell, muttered a prayer and squeezed the trigger.

Stirwell never stood a chance. He went down a bloodied mess. Unrecognizable for she'd blasted off his head. For once in his life Jess knew what to do. He dived for the cast-iron horse trough. Not that the other two were thinking of him right now. They were too busy trying to remain seated as their horses reared and plunged.

"Get the hell out of here."

To Jess's disbelief they rode out. The gun fired again but Clementine missed.

"Hell!" Jess exclaimed in disbelief. He could not believe he was still alive. And Stirwell was lying there dead. To a degree poor old Mat had been avenged. And, despite the sword which still hung over his head, Jess felt considerably cheered. Magnalia had come to Capra expecting to have an easy time of it. Expecting to have things all his own way. Well this time, maybe, just maybe, Magnalia's luck would run out on him. Jess prayed that it would. Prayed that it would before Magnalia sought retribution for Stirwell.

* * *

Gracie had told him that if he poked his nose into the Red Garter she would shoot it off. Clay stared at the cell wall. He was missing her company. She was one hell of a woman and he'd never meet another like her.

"I said," Gaskill snapped, "I said when the hell are you going to get out of my jail?"

"Huh!" Clay turned his head. An irate Gaskill stood framed in the doorway.

"Church funds don't run to hotel bills," Clay rejoined. "Fact is in the circumstances the parishioners are supposed to offer board and lodging." He paused. "There ain't none of them offered!" He swung his legs off the bunk. "This place is as good as any.

It was here or the livery barn. Put the coffee on. You've got the sugar in, ain't you?"

"Sure," Gaskill grumbled. It could have been worse. The Reverend Clay Purnell could have been concerning himself about the range war which was undoubtably brewing but the only thing on Purnell's mind seemed to be the state of Miss Gracie's temper and sugar for the coffee. And that was good because a range war was a dirty business. And it was not possible to stop it. All anyone could do was ride it out.

He put two steaming-hot mugs of coffee down on the cigarette-scarred desk. Absentmindedly Clay pulled up a chair. "I aim to marry Gracie," he stated. "And, as I ain't exactly welcome in this town, I aim to move on. I'm requesting a new posting. Gracie hates this damn town. I can't ask her to stay here." He grinned. "That's settled."

"Good. I reckon you've made the right decision." Gaskill was reaching out to shake Clay's hand when the door of his office burst open. Magnalia, his expression ugly, strode into the office.

His bloodshot eyes came to rest upon Clay Purnell. "Get the hell out of here, Preacher," he ordered contemptuously.

Clay stayed put. He resisted an urge to punch Magnalia in the teeth. Clay didn't take kindly to being addressed as though he were a dog. In the old days he would have busted Magnalia. Now of course he must strive to turn the other cheek.

"Don't mind him none," Gaskill replied offhandedly. "He lives here. I take it you've come to see me upon urgent business."

"You've heard ain't you? About Stirwell? My ramrod. Gunned down in cold blood."

"Sure I've heard," Gaskill rejoined.

"I want that woman arrested for murder."

"That woman has got eight young ones," Clay observed. "And expecting another although it don't show yet."

He took a drink of coffee. "And I reckon she was provoked."

"No one gives a damn what you think, Preacher."

"I ain't arresting her," Gaskill stated. "Stirwell, now, he was a gunhand. It's only right and natural he died by the gun. He ought to have taken account of the fact that there was a woman inside with a gun. He made a mistake. He paid the price."

"You took my money. We made a deal."

"So we did," Gaskill agreed, unabashed. "I agreed to keep out of it when you and Brewes started swapping lead and that's what I aim to do. It don't matter a damn to me which one of you kills the other." He smirked. "I've got my rep to think of. I've brought in," he hesitated, "leastways killed," he amended, "some real hardcases, and now you expect me to go out after Clementine White. Next thing you'll be telling me to house the young ones in my jailhouse and deliver the baby." He actually grinned with amusement.

"Why you two-time skunk!" Magnalia exploded.

There was an ominous silence. When Gaskill spoke his voice was unnaturally low. "Get out of here before I kill you. The deal is off right now. I'll be watching you like a hawk, Magnalia. You make one wrong move and I'll have you." He tapped his badge. "I've got right on my side. Hell, if you think you're dealing with some has-been, two-bit lawman you've got a lot to learn. I ain't gunned anyone since I've been in Capra. Shoot off your mouth again and you'll be my first." He stood up. "And leave that woman be. If she meets up with an accident I'll know where to look."

Magnalia opened his mouth as though to speak. Thought better of it and then retreated.

"Hell," Gaskill exclaimed. "I'm a louse but I won't have a woman in my jail."

Clay stood up. He had feared for a moment Gaskill would go after Clementine. "The damn thing is I'll be officiating at Stirwell's burial. Him and old Mat. I guess I'm stumped for words this time." He moved towards the door. "I guess this time Magnalia has bitten off more than he can chew. He'll miss Stirwell. Magnalia's kind always relies upon the Stirwells of the world. Maybe the loss will slow him down for a while. Put a spoke in the wheel. But the outcome of this fracas ain't going to be my concern. Not this time." He shrugged. "Maybe you'll surprise us all, Gaskill, and turn into an honest lawman."

"Get lost, Preacher," Gaskill responded good-naturedly.

* * *

Magnalia had always prided himself on being a fair judge of a man. Gaskill was a man with violent tendencies. The rancher had known that another careless word could send Gaskill over the edge. And, as Gaskill had said, right was on his side. He was the one with a badge. If he wanted to shoot a man down and say after the event that man had made to draw his gun no one would argue.

Certainly not that no-account preacher. Magnalia cursed loudly. He'd have them both removed. Killed. Not immediately. He'd bring in a hired gun. The best there was. A man who'd be a match for that little runt of a lawman and the meddling preacher. Both of them could stay in Capra permanently. Six feet under in the town's cemetery.

Filled with fury the mean-hearted man rode his horse mercilessly, taking out his rage on the long-suffering animal. Silver-star spurs thudded viciously into the animal's flanks, for no other reason than Magnalia wanted to inflict pain. On anything. And the horse was handy.

And that needless act of cruelty

saved his life. A rifle spat viciously. At the same time the pain-maddened animal reared up unseating his rider. The rifle spat again. A bullet thudded into the horse. With a scream it went down trapping Magnalia's legs beneath heaving flanks. Screams filled the air. Screams from Magnalia and screams from the horse. And then a further bullet mercifully put the horse out of its misery.

Brewes, it had to be Brewes, or one of his trusted men up there amongst the acclivities taking pot-shots. Another bullet struck dirt near to Magnalia's head.

Brewes had out-smarted him. Made the first move. Hell, the first thing he ought to have done was set up an ambush to get Brewes. Jess White could have waited. Brewes ought to have been the first target. He could see it now. He'd underestimated the man.

And now all Brewes had to do was to come down from the rocks and put a bullet into his victim's head. He could not be stopped. Magnalia was helpless and knew it.

"You yellow bastard," he screamed. "You ain't got the guts to face me man to man. Show yourself."

No one moved. It did not occur to Magnalia that if his assailant had been John Brewes it was not very likely the man would have botched the job.

"Lord help me. Lord help me," Magnalia sobbed.

Magnalia's assailant was also sobbing but for a different reason. She'd failed. And she hadn't been brave enough to go down and put a bullet into his head. And now it was too late, a wagon was coming. And if Gaskill found out about this he'd throw her in jail. But she didn't regret what she'd tried to do. She was only sorry she'd hit the poor horse. On hands and knees, keeping down so she wouldn't be spotted Clementine White crawled away. She wouldn't give up. If she stayed free she'd have another try. She had to. Sooner or later he'd have Jess blasted and take the ranch.

Even though he did not see signs of movement the dirt-farmer who'd arrived to save Magnalia's hide fired at the rocks. If the man had possessed a grain of sense he would have realized that he made an excellent target himself and more importantly he would have been best advised to climb aboard his wagon and leave the man he'd chanced upon for the buzzards.

However, not knowing Magnalia's nature, the man set to rescuing the trapped man. And it was no easy task hauling the dead horse off its rider. First, the oxen had to be unhitched from the wagon and then hitched to the horse. And all the while the rancher cursed and sobbed with pain alternately.

The woman wrung her hands while her husband rambled on heedless whether the man could hear him.

"Heard tell there's free range east of Cougar's Bluff. That's where we're headed. I aim to irrigate. Plant my crops and rear my young ones. Now don't you feel beholden. I don't want no payment for doing a neighbourly turn. Can we take you anywhere, mister?"

Magnalia mumbled directions for the Twisted M ranch. Cougar's Bluff was on Twisted M range. He'd have no damn dirt-farmer stringing wire on Twisted M range, building a damn dugout, ploughing up the land.

Just before he passed out Magnalia dredged up the name he'd been looking for. Flick. That was the man he wanted. Flick was the fastest gun for hire that there was. If anyone could outgun Gaskill and the preacher it would be Flick.

9

"WELL I guess the range war has been postponed," Gaskill spoke with dry humour. "Word is Magnalia's legs were smashed up pretty bad. Doc ain't certain he'll get back the use of them. Let's hope he don't." He frowned. "It ain't like John Brewes to miss. That don't set right. 'Less it was not his original intention to kill him. And it couldn't have been Two Bits. If ever a man deserved his sobriquet it's Jess White!" He cut himself a plug of chewing tobacco. "Feel like a game of chess?"

"Nope. And if I were you, Gaskill, I'd not get complacent. There's talk over at the Cattlemen's Association. Talk about an influx of dirt-farmers and what they aim to do about it. John Brewes is over there right now, whipping up feelings. The word vigilantes is being mentioned."

"How'd you know?" Gaskill grinned. "You've been at the saloon sparking Gracie. How'd you get on?"

Clay shrugged. "She wouldn't give me the time of day. Shut herself in her room as soon as I came in."

"Well, for the Lord's sake you ought to have busted down her door. Women like a strong man. Don't tell me you ain't got what it takes to win Miss Gracie's heart? Clay Purnell, I'm sorely disappointed in you."

"And you ain't one wit worried about vigilantes!"

"Nope. You ought to be wearing a badge, Clay. You seem damn keen to do my job."

Clay stood up.

"And I reckon you're going to snoop around. See if you can find tracks leading from the scene of the shooting to John Brewes' land. That ain't proof. It counts for nothing. Heard tell Mrs Brewes and her daughter bought tickets for Boston. I wonder how she got round him? It ain't like Brewes to be over generous with money."

"Ask your wife if you're that curious," Clay muttered. The hell of it was Gaskill's kind of law-keeping suited the cattlemen just fine. He scowled. And, as for Magnalia being finished as Gaskill seemed to believe, well, Clay wasn't sure about that. And damn it Gaskill was right. He ought to have busted in Gracie's door. But at the time it had not seemed the way to set about proposing.

On the way out of town he passed John Brewes standing outside the hotel. Brewes actually smiled as though enjoying a private joke. And that smile made Clay feel damn uneasy.

John Brewes watched the preacher ride out of town. Purnell did not know it yet but his days in Capra were numbered. The man had to be got rid of. When the trouble came Brewes believed Purnell would side with the dirt-farmers. Stand up alongside them.

Purnell might not like dirt-farmers but his conscience would not let him stand idle whilst farmers were harried, maybe gunned down if that was what it took to stop them blighting the land. For once every member of the Association was in agreement.

Purnell was to be removed. And not one hair of his head would suffer. As Mrs Brewes had pointed out violence wasn't the way to have the minister removed. Purnell didn't know it but he was due to be ordered overseas. The town council had given the man a glowing recommendation. Hardworking, toiling endlessly for the good of others, Purnell was about to get his just reward. And all thanks to Mrs Brewes. As she'd said, the Reverend Purnell had to answer to higher authority and he had to obey orders.

* * *

Gracie surveyed her leg. Clad in a black silk stocking she considered it to be a mighty fine leg. But not fine enough to keep Clay Purnell. The fact that she'd asked Clay Purnell to marry her had become the town joke. At least as far as she was concerned. She didn't think anyone would be fool enough to crack any jokes within Clay's hearing but she was another matter.

The men especially. More than one had said within her hearing that although Clay Purnell was undoubtedly a darn fool he was not that much of a fool. The men had sniggered. The women sniffed and one had declared loudly, as Gracie was passing by, "I'm sure when the minister does get married he'll find himself a respectable woman."

The barb had hurt more than she cared to admit. Dropping her skirt she lit herself a cigar. She'd made a darn fool of herself that was for sure. And she was weary of Capra. Hell, she'd had a bellyful of this town she thought with a flash of old spirit. She'd never been one to feel sorry for herself. She shrugged. Clay Purnell could go to the devil, or stay in Capra. As for herself she was moving on. It was high time. True she hadn't much of a stake but it was enough to get her out of Capra.

Stage was leaving today. She pulled down her battered suitcase. She'd seen a lot of towns. But something told her she'd always remember this one. And its preacher for he was a man worth remembering.

Whilst Gracie was packing her suitcase Clay was scouring the acclivities overlooking the spot Magnalia had been drygulched. It had been easy to pinpoint the exact spot. The bleaching bones of Magnalia's horse, now picked clean, spoke for themselves.

He found what he'd been looking for. The evidence which confirmed his suspicions. A scrap of gingham upon a thorn bush. He'd agreed with Gaskill, Two Bits wasn't the man for this kind of work and Brewes would not have botched the job. And womenfolk were not to be underestimated. Gracie had taught him that.

Clay put the gingham in his pocket. He knew who'd gunned down Magnalia but he'd keep the knowledge to himself. Clementine White had done what she had to do. He couldn't blame her. Her secret was safe.

Clay wiped the sweat from his brow. It was hot. Hotter than hell. Tempers frayed and gave in this kind of heat. He felt uneasy. So maybe he'd mosey on to Two Bits' spread and find out whether Two Bits had received any threats. If there'd been incidents he didn't know about such as slaughtered cattle or anything else of that nature. Maybe he'd stay the night. He'd noticed two of Magnalia's men standing over Stirwell's grave, drinking and swearing, men who had not attended the burying but nevertheless were paying their respects in their own kind of way.

True, Magnalia had been warned to leave the Whites be but Magnalia was a mad dog and so were the men who worked for him. Magnalia had recruited scum and that was a fact.

* * *

Brewes knew that more or less he had the Association with him. But there still remained a few Doubting Thomases. The spokes in the wheel were Gaskill and the minister.

The door had been bolted and a guard placed outside. Now the smoke-filled room was thick with conspiracy and for once the members of the Cattlemen's Association were in accord, something had to be done about the damn farmers. Brewes had the stage. Magnalia, laid up with crippled legs was yesterday's man. True it had looked at one time as though Magnalia would displace Brewes as head man at the Association but the danger was past.

"Purnell is moving on," the rancher declared, "so there's no cause to worry about him. He don't know it yet. Mrs Brewes worked damn hard to get it done. She corresponds with all manner of folk. Some of them useful!" He paused. "Purnell's heading for London, England. They're sending him overseas."

Someone guffawed, and commented, "Well there ain't nothing to keep him in Capra. Gracie pulled out. Boarded the stage this afternoon. He'll get no more nights at the Red Garter. Those girls work by the minute."

At that there was a spate of ribald comments concerning Clay Purnell's proclivities.

"What do you think he'll do?" the question was addressed to no one in particular.

"Damn it! He'll follow orders of course," Brewes snapped.

"I mean about Gracie."

"He'll not trouble about a no-account floozie," Brewes gritted, patience thin. "Now, gentlemen, if we can just get back to business."

"I'm betting he'll go after her." The rancher MacDougal ignored John

Brewes. And then to John Brewes' disgust bets were laid and further lewd comments made.

"Gentlemen!" He brought his fist down upon the table. "I'm willing to bet! On Gaskill. That our good sheriff won't do a damn thing about any nightriders."

"You can't be sure of that, Brewes." MacDougal was in an argumentative mood. "Until I'm convinced I ain't about to lock horns with that murderously inclined bastard. You ought never to have brought him to Capra."

"Have a cigar, MacDougal." Brewes concealed his anger. "Tomorrow we'll know." He paused. "Dirtbusters ain't the only enemy as Two Bits will vouch. I'm fixing it that if Gaskill goes after anyone on account of tonight's work it'll be Magnalia. The man aims to expand; work on us one by one till he's kingpin around here. Well, this time he ain't having things his way. Fact is, gents, I've been doing some checking on friend Magnalia." He then proceeded to recount the various endeavours he'd so far learned about. By the time he'd finished speaking they were with him.

* * *

Two Bits was on edge. The man could not have hidden his unease even if his life had depended on it. Clementine was calm enough. Predictably Clay had been invited for supper. The Whites sure as hell disapproved of him but good manners had prevailed. So, Clay had found himself sitting down to a meal of fried pork and beans together with fresh-baked bread. Then Clementine had prevailed upon him to read from the Bible whilst she darned the socks and Two Bits' unease grew.

Did Two Bits know what she'd done Clay wondered. Was Two Bits expecting trouble? Maybe. The man looked guilty. Clay had learned to recognize the signs. Decent folk were always feeling guilty about something or other. Clementine, not reckoning she'd done wrong, now she looked at ease. Not so her husband.

"Read on, Minister," Clementine urged.

Clay read on. And then he heard it. Distant but unmistakable. The sound of stampeding cattle. That was something every drover feared. The stampede. Clay had seen some good men die beneath hooked, lethal horns.

Clementine White sprang up in alarm but Two Bits stayed seated. "Stay put, Mother," he advised. "They'll not be headed this way."

Clementine stared at her husband glass-eyed with fear. "That'll be Magnalia beef," she blurted out oblivious to the thunderous look her husband gave her. "There's a fair parcel of them on our land. What's happening, Jess?"

"Damned if I know, Mother," her husband lied. "Sit tight, Minister. There's no need to trouble yourself none." He spoke without looking Clay in the eye.

"I'll be the judge of that." Clay eyed Two Bits speculatively and then headed for the door. Outside the night was cool. A magnitude of stars lit the sky. Tilting his head Clay tried to determine the direction of the stampede. And the distant gunshots. He thinned his lips. Men fired guns to get the critters moving not to stop them. He headed towards the barn knowing that he was duty bound to find out the reason behind the stampede.

* * *

"I reckon Mr Magnalia's beholden to us. We know it. He knows it." There was a note of satisfaction in the man's voice. "How's the chicken doing, Wife?"

"Won't cook no faster for asking," she replied wearily. She'd been the one to make the fire, pluck the chickens, make the biscuits, milk the cow. True he'd made a start on the dugout but she was sick of hearing about how he'd saved Mr Magnalia. And, after she'd served up, there'd be damn little chicken for her to eat.

"Land's big enough for both of us," the man continued. "Serve up that chicken will you? I'm through waiting." His stomach growled.

She reached for the chicken and then froze. There came the sound of thunder. And something else. Gunshots. Whooping and shouting. "Lord almighty, they're coming this way."

* * *

To say that there'd been nothing personal in the choice of example would have been a lie. Brewes had purposely settled on the squatters camped out at the Bluff. Not solely because they were on Magnalia's doorstep: he bore the darn fool of a farmer a grudge. The man had saved Magnalia and thus occasioned every decent rancher in Capra a whole lot of trouble, himself included.

And, as Two Bits had said, the cattle were placed most convenient to the Bluffs. A whole bunch of Magnalia steers ready and waiting, grazing on Two Bits' land. Just waiting to be returned to Mr Magnalia himself and if they were to stampede through Cougar's Bluff and if a damned fool dirtbuster was camped out at the Bluff then that was too darn bad.

Conscience clear, John Brewes led the night-riders himself. To him the dirtbusters with their huge broods of ragged youngsters were worse than chisellers, prairie dogs ruining the land and the men who ranched that land, decent good men who'd fought Indians and owlhoots, drought and freezing snow, paid for the land in blood and were now expected to give way to the encroaching little men with their wagons and milk cow and their ploughs.

Clay reached the scene of destruction

as night gave way to day. There was nothing much left, it being nigh impossible even to tell how many had died under the hooves of the cattle. The remains were mangled, scraps of people, people who'd come West full of hope and had ended like this. There were tears in his eyes as he covered the pathetic remnants of the people they'd been with stones. Bowing his head he knelt down and prayed for those who had died and for those who had done it.

Two Bits had known about this. And gone along with it. Most likely then Magnalia hadn't been the one responsible. That left Brewes and the rest of the Association. Anger and sadness filled him as he rode back to Capra. Those who had done this evil ought to pay. He dismounted before the sheriff's office thinking that Gaskill wouldn't give a damn about all this.

"Satisfied your curiosity?" Gaskill asked as Clay came in. And then, as he caught sight of Clay's expression,

"Hell! What's troubling you, man? You're a mite green around the gills ain't you? I saw a man pole-axed once and you've got that same kind of glass-eyed look."

Briefly Clay told him of his discovery at Cougar's Bluff. Gaskill listened in silence. His expression remained unaltered.

"And now you're feeling sorry for the farmers. Save your sympathy you damn fool." He shrugged. "Hell, I'll deal with the nightriders. A few well-chosen words over at the Association will halt those bastards in their tracks."

"What words?" Clay asked curiously, surprised that Gaskill was going to get up off his butt and do something about the situation that was developing.

Gaskill grinned. "Words to the effect that if the nightriders ride again I aim to put all their names into my hand and draw out one name to go after. Words to the effect that Mrs Gaskill's brother is commander over at the fort. And he owes me. Words to the effect that when

I step on toes, them there unfortunate folk lose their toes." He shrugged. "Read this. That ought to surprise you some." Carelessly he tossed the package to Clay. "See the address."

Clay glanced at the address. "How come you've got this?"

He perused the missive his frown deepening. He felt as though he'd been kicked in the gut.

"Solomon!" Gaskill's grin was feral. "I make a point of knowing what's going on in my town, Preacher. Well, what do you say now you know them sanctimonious dirtbusters are doing their damnest not only to get you removed but to get your collar removed likewise, on account of your debauched behaviour, consorting with loose women. That's Gracie I reckon. Not that you'll be doing any further consorting seeing she's upped and quit town." He shook his head. "Fact is, Clay, you'll be moving on in any event. Some place that needs your zeal. Mrs Brewes now, she's got connections.

She's gone and recommended you most highly. Of course them damn dirtbusters ain't aware of it!"

"You aim to take care of the nightriders?" Clay repeated, unable to quite believe the sheriff.

"I said so didn't I?" Gaskill responded, a mite irritated by Clay's disbelief.

Clay nodded. "Fair enough," he rejoined. "You know where Gracie's headed?"

"Sure," Gaskill responded. "What's it to you?"

"I aim to go after her," Clay responded. He shrugged. "After that I guess I'll just have to wait on learning where those high up have elected to send me. Guess I'll be hearing soon enough."

"You surely will." Gaskill looked as though he'd like to say more. "Maybe some place where you won't need your Peacemaker."

"Maybe. Now if you'll tell me where Gracie's bound for I'll hit the trail."

With a grin Gaskill relayed the

information. “Clay,” he concluded with a wink.

“Yup.” Clay paused at the door.

“Do your damnest to stay out of trouble,” the sheriff advised. “It’s asking a lot but do your best.” As the door closed Gaskill couldn’t help but think that trouble and Clay Purnell seemed to go together.

10

CLAY rode out of Capra. It stuck in his craw that folk who'd wished him howdy and good day had conspired against him, conspired not only to have him removed but also thrown out of the church. He made a note of those names and they'd been farmers every one.

He shrugged. What the hell. He was being run out of town, moved on. A man would have hired a killer but women often had other ways. Mrs Brewes had done what neither her husband or Magnalia could have done. Forced him out before he was ready to leave.

And he sure as hell hoped Gracie's temper had cooled by the time he caught up with her. For the life of him he could not understand why she'd upped and quit without a word to him.

* * *

The boss of the Birdcage was a mean-eyed *hombre* called Mills. And he was vastly different from the last man she'd worked for. Gracie had a hunch that the girls were afraid of the varmint. Planting her hands on her hips she squared up to her new boss.

"I ain't going up in one of your damn birdcages," she declared.

Her boss in Capra wouldn't have pressed the point. So you ain't going up he would have said and left it at that. Fact was her last boss would never have come up with the idea of hanging human-size birdcages from the ceiling. Cages designed to house the girls. They were the birds. And for a sizeable fee a customer could join a girl in a birdcage, draw the curtains and have himself a good time swinging from the ceiling.

Why if Clay were to come in and see her sitting up there in a birdcage she'd never be able to look him in the eye again. But who was she fooling?

He wouldn't come after her. Most likely he was glad to find her gone. And she was damned if she'd sit in a birdcage. "I ain't going up." She made to turn away.

A hand shot out. Nails dug into her flesh. "I give the orders around here you . . ."

The name he called her riled her plenty. "You do." The nails dug deeper. Gracie reached behind her for the whiskey bottle which stood on the bar. "You do!" she repeated bringing her arm forward. The bottle came down with a thud.

Two things happened simultaneously. "You're for it now, Gracie. He's got the judge in his pocket," one of the girls squawked, looking at Gracie in plain disbelief. Those words would have got Gracie out of town save for the fact that the sheriff chose that moment to come through the batwings. "Hell!" Gracie exclaimed. A few moments later she wished she was back in Capra. Leastways Gaskill wouldn't have put her under lock and key.

And right now she would have given anything to see Clay Purnell. He might not want to marry her but he would not have seen them railroad her.

As the cell door slammed shut behind Gracie, Clay, although he hadn't exactly found trouble had sure as hell found something. He knelt beside the man he'd chanced upon. There was a faint pulse and the man, whoever he was, wasn't dead, leastways not yet.

The victim had been back shot. Clay swore explicitly. In his opinion back shooting was as low as a man could get. Carefully he turned the man over. The face which looked up at him was almost boyish. As low as a man could get even when the victim was one Isaac Flick, gun for hire, indiscriminate young killer who deserved to be blasted.

And deserved to be left where he'd fallen. Ride on a silent voice prompted. Clay thinned his lips. Hell, he was sorely tempted. If thanks to Clay's intervention Isaac Flick pulled through he'd go on to kill again, and yet to leave the murderous son of a bitch didn't set right either.

He didn't know what to do. He was stumped. He stared down at Flick. Flick's eyes opened, focusing on Clay's stiff white collar. Flick forced the words out with considerable difficulty. "You go to hell Bible thumper," he croaked. "I don't want no help from the likes of you." His eyes closed.

Clay considered the unconscious man. Maybe this was a test of sorts. He made a decision. "Well you no-good, little bastard you're going to get my help." Providently he had the means to help Isaac Flick packed away in his gunny sack. He never travelled without them. Now he had to doctor Isaac Flick.

He fetched the vial of carbolic acid and the long thin skewer needed to probe Flick's flesh and locate that bullet.

As he was not kindly disposed towards Flick it would be easier to ignore the pain he'd have to inflict. Nevertheless Clay took a slug of whiskey before he started work having first tied Flick down. If Flick died during the operation, or even shortly afterwards, life would be simpler. If Flick lived he'd be needing a place. Somewhere he could lie up and recuperate.

Sweat dotted Clay's brow as he got on with the grisly task. A while back he'd passed a stage depot, run by a woman of all things. He guessed she'd take in Isaac Flick if she were paid enough. Clay's conscience smote him. It didn't seem right to leave Flick with an unsuspecting woman although the only folk Flick killed were those he'd been paid to kill. Flick didn't go looking for trouble for the sake of trouble and there'd never been any talk about Flick molesting females. Clay guessed he'd have to tell the woman the truth and let her decide.

Clay felt for Flick's pulse and to his disappointment found it. He thinned his lips. There it was beating away and he had a hunch that Isaac Flick, despite the odds, would keep on breathing. And his own journey had now been delayed. Of necessity he must wait to see what happened, see whether he needed to build a travois to haul Flick to the depot or dig a grave to bury the varmint.

* * *

It was the chink of coins which penetrated Flick's unconscious state. His eyes felt as though they were weighted down. He struggled to lift his lids, eventually succeeding. He was in, of all places, a bed. His nostrils flared. He smelt that smell peculiar to freshly laundered and dried sheets. He could smell bread baking. Three people stood alongside the bed, a man, a woman and a boy.

And the woman was wearing man's

clothes. And toting a Peacemaker. Isaac Flick was truly shocked!

"Well he don't look nothing special!" The boy sounded disappointed.

The woman snorted. "He ain't nothing special," she declared. "Dirt that's what he is." And then added hurriedly, "Don't you worry none, Reverend Purnell, you'll not be cheated. I'll keep my word. I'll tend this varmint until he's willing to ride out. Now don't you feel guilty about leaving him in my charge. I can tell you're fretting to get on after your fiancée."

"I surely am," the minister spoke. "But . . . "

"I'll be safe enough. If he shows any signs of being a danger to me or my brother I'll blast him. That's fair enough, ain't it?"

"Sure," Clay agreed. "Don't stand there thinking about it. Just do it."

"I sure will. I ain't a fool."

"Riders coming in, Sis. Two of them."

"And coming in fast." She'd crossed

to the window. "Don't appear to me like casual callers. Could this have anything to do with the varmint you've brought in?" There was a pause. "Someone back shot him. We don't know why or who but maybe . . . "

"I'd best handle this, ma'am. Stay inside."

"What do you aim to do?"

"I don't know. See how the cards fall I guess. I'm loath to shoot two decent men on account of this varmint."

"Decent men!" she snorted. "There's precious few of them about. Yourself excluded, of course, Reverend."

Isaac Flick tried to raise himself up but fell back after lifting himself just an inch. If the two riding in were the two he suspected them to be then Clay Purnell's doctoring had been in vain.

Clay Purnell, Minister of Capra. Life paid the damnest tricks. He'd been heading for Capra. Word was that he was wanted there urgent by one Magnalia. There were three men Magnalia wanted taken out:

a rancher answering to the name of John Brewes; the sheriff, Gaskill; and, of all things, the town's minister, one Clay Purnell. Flick had harboured reservations against taking out the minister, it not seeming right to gun down a man unacquainted with the handling of a Peacemaker.

Well, Clay Purnell, as he wore a Peacemaker tied low at the hip was obviously more than acquainted with the Peacemaker. If he lived Flick knew he'd have to turn Magnalia's generous offer down flat. It went against his principles to gun down a man who'd saved his life. And he was damned if he'd do it, not for any price.

"Tell me." His throat worked as he struggled to continue. "What's happening?" he croaked. The kid, naturally enough, was at the window. The woman had quit the room.

"It looks like gunplay," the kid piped cheerfully, not troubling to turn his head. "One of them is a shouting and waving his arms."

"What they look like kid?"

"Well, they ain't smiling," the kid replied, missing the question.

Flick groaned. "Is one of them bald?"

"Like a baby," came the answer.

Ossie. One of them was Ossie. That meant the other one was Johnny Chequer. Chequer had picked a fight and the two of them had faced up to one another on Main Street. Flick, however, unfortunately had been careless. He hadn't reckoned on Ossie being squirrelled away at an upstairs window overlooking Main Street. It had been Ossie's shot which had brought him down. Chequer had missed. Unfortunately the slug meant for Chequer had gone wide Ossie's slug having deflected his aim.

The bastards had come after him. He hadn't expected that. But with Chequer he might have known it. He lay there helpless unable to quite believe that the Reverend Clay Purnell aimed to take on the two gunmen.

Clay saw straight off that the sight of his dog collar had flummoxed the two hardcases who'd confidently dismounted before the depot. Two unsavoury-looking hardcases, he corrected as the silence dragged on, they evidently anticipating that he'd be the first to break it.

He held his peace. He didn't scare nor did he gabble away like a fool.

The silence lasted a mite longer, then the taller of the men laughed, revealing teeth which put Clay in mind of a rabbit. His lips twitched with amusement.

"No call for alarm, Reverend," the buck teeth advised, mistaking the twitching for fear. He sounded satisfied. Clay guessed the man liked to see others sweat. "I guess that explains it," buck teeth continued, "only a dog collar would trouble himself with the likes of Isaac Flick."

"Perhaps he ain't heard of Isaac Flick," his companion a bald-headed *hombre* with a mouth filled with gold teeth commented. The remark was not well received.

"For the Lord's sake, Ossie, everyone has heard of Isaac Flick. I'm Johnny Chequer!" Unexpectedly he introduced himself, eyes watching for Clay's reaction.

"Johnny Chequer!" Clay mused. "Yup. I've heard of you."

Johnny Chequer was an up-and-coming gunman. From the satisfaction spread over Chequer's face Clay guessed his response was the one Chequer had wanted. He'd said the right words, not that he gave a damn about placating Johnny Chequer, low-down killer.

"I reckon you might have." There was a pause. "I gunned down Isaac Flick fair and square." His eyes challenged Clay to dispute the obvious lie.

Clay held his tongue. Whether Flick had been gunned down fair and square was not the moot point here.

"And he's been photographed alongside the body," Ossie broke in eagerly.

Clay shrugged. "Seems to me," he drawled, "a man can only be labelled a body when he's good and dead."

"That's true," Ossie agreed. "The bastard fooled us. We thought he was dead. Weren't no sign of life. I couldn't find . . . "

"Fact is," Chequer snarled, "my damn fool of a pard made a mistake."

Clay shook his head. Words failed him.

"We're here to take the body back to town," Ossie continued. "Paper won't print the damn story without the body. Verification it's him and he's dead."

"How'd you lose the body?" Clay drawled. "Mighty careless of you weren't it?"

"Bastard crawled out of town whilst I was treating folk to a whiskey," Chequer rejoined. "Fact is Ossie was told to tote Flick over to the undertakers, fact is Ossie just left Flick lying out on Main Street. Now, stand aside, Minister, and I'll tote him back to town. This time I aim to deliver him personally. There won't be no slip up." He laughed. "As you say there ain't exactly a body lying in there." He jerked his head towards the building. "But there will be mighty soon."

"Why'd you want to kill Isaac Flick?" Clay enquired mildly, making no move to step aside. Whatever he elected to do next hinged on Chequer's answer. He reckoned it would be a straight answer. Chequer would not lie. He would not see a reason to lie. If Chequer had had good reason to kill Flick, revenge for a wrong that had been done, that made a good deal of difference.

"Huh!" Chequer looked at Clay as if he'd been found wanting. He grinned. "I reckon you don't understand such matters, Preacher. Why else would I want to kill him other than to enhance my rep."

"Then he ain't killed no one near and dear to you?" Clay persisted.

Both men guffawed. "Hell no. Ain't I just said?" Chequer exclaimed, clearly nonplussed.

"Then I ain't stepping aside," Clay responded. He knew what was coming and knew he could not avoid gunplay. "The enhancement of your rep ain't reason enough. You've had a wasted ride, gents. I ain't able to oblige."

"What!" Chequer's lips compressed into a thin line. Spots of colour stained pallid cheeks. The man was angry. "Flick ain't worth dying for." He forced the words out, evidently finding it hard to control his anger.

"You ain't never said a truer word," Clay rejoined. "Don't either of you die on account of Isaac Flick."

Chequer's restraint snapped. "You damn fool. I ain't talking about myself. I was giving you one last chance on account of that damn collar. You've misread the situation, Preacher. I'm counting to ten and if you ain't moved you're dead meat!"

Clay stood firm. Chequer and Ossie reached on the count of seven. He was not caught unaware. He'd been prepared for a double cross. Neither of the two had possessed much savvy. They positioned themselves in such a way that the sunlight struck their eyes. They shot 'blind' and missed.

As Chequer's hand had flashed down his own hand had reached. Now he stood holding his smoking Peacemaker staring down at two dead men. The smell of gunsmoke lingered in the air, a smell he never seemed able to get away from.

"I've got to bury them. Here." He spoke to the woman who'd come out from the house. "Naturally if anyone enquires tell them the truth." He hesitated. "Fact is I don't want to be labelled the man who gunned down Johnny Chequer." He touched his collar. "This makes it damn tricky and . . . " He hesitated. "And I want to enjoy married life without having every would-be fast gun knocking on my door."

"Sounds reasonable enough," the woman agreed. "Why didn't you let them have him?"

"I'm a fool I guess." Clay took the shovel the woman brought out from the house. "Knowing what's right ain't easy." The shovel struck earth. He was eager now to ride on after Gracie. Hell he wouldn't allow himself to dwell on what Gracie might be doing this very moment. He didn't like the idea of her entertaining anyone other than himself.

"Mind you don't break my damn shovel!"

The woman's voice brought him back to reality. Clay got himself under control. With his own abysmal record he was in no position to condemn Gracie; killing folk was a damn sight worse than entertaining them. He guessed he'd better remind himself of that fact whenever he felt himself grow hot under the collar.

* * *

Gracie bristled with suppressed fury. Folk had come to the so-called Court

House to be entertained. Some of them had even brought picnic baskets along with the fried chicken and lemonade for the day was hot and the lemonade much appreciated. The women in their faded ginghams were here to learn about the goings on within the Birdcage saloon and to see one of the creatures who worked in the Birdcage get her just deserts.

The trial was a joke from its start to its conclusion, and the verdict surprised her not a wit.

They found her guilty.

She steeled herself for the verdict but was nevertheless caught unprepared. Ten years in the penitentiary for attempted murder. Reeling from the shock of it she stared at the judge. She'd been railroaded. No one expected her to do anything. The overweight, indolent sheriff failed to react as she leapt to her feet, overturned the table at which she was sitting and headed for the judge.

Pandemonium broke out. What happened next gave the town something to talk about for months to come, leastways the womenfolk fortunate to be present that day.

The lawman made no attempt to draw his weapon or to move his bulk from his chair. Fact was no one made an attempt to apprehend the prisoner. The huge belly of the lawman shook with amusement as he watched the woman attack the judge, and she knew how to make good use of a clenched fist and a long nail.

Once the furious woman had been restrained the result was inevitable.

"Prison is no place for this woman. She needs committing," the judge, shaken up as he was, could hardly mouth the words.

Gracie's shrieks when she heard herself committed indefinitely to the asylum echoed clear down Main Street.

11

THE lamp cast shadows upon the wall. The room was but dimly lit. Magnalia did not want to be seen clearly. Now he downed yet another tumbler of cheap whiskey in one gulp. A surfeit of whiskey, he had found, deadened the pain which constantly troubled him night and day.

Although how the hell a man who'd been told he would not walk again could feel pain was beyond him. He'd asked that question many times taking hope from the pain. It proved to him that he damn well would walk again and the sawbones did not know what he was talking about.

The doc's manner had been brusque. Magnalia reckoned the no-account doctor had taken pleasure in delivering his verdict. Pompous old jackass

Magnalia thought. He didn't give a damn what the old fool said. He'd show them all. Damn right he would.

The 'all' were the members of the Cattlemen's Association, men who'd drunk his whiskey and now, when he was laid low, had seized the opportunity to cancel his membership. That the move was the work of John Brewes, Magnalia did not doubt. For Brewes had possessed the gall to ride out to Magnalia's ranch house and deliver the news personally.

And to make him an offer.

An offer to buy him out.

Brewes was here now, legs firmly planted, refusing to sit, preferring to stand because that way he was able to look down upon the man he'd conspired against. And Brewes had sworn on the dog-eared Bible he'd toted along with him that he'd had no hand in or knowledge of the bushwhacking. "That ain't my way," he'd said.

John Brewes shifted from foot to foot. He'd waited a long time whilst

Magnalia considered the offer, a fair offer, one which Magnalia, if he possessed a grain of sense, would take. A man couldn't run a spread if he was confined to a chair. Already Magnalia's crew were taking full advantage of their boss's affliction. The saloons and whores of Capra had been seeing a good deal of Magnalia's crew. A fair number of them were even now in town enjoying themselves, the remainder were laid up at the bunkhouse swilling cheap whiskey and card playing.

"Face it man." John Brewes decided it was time for straight talking. "You're finished in Capra and you can't go on pretending otherwise. The whole town knows you ain't never going to walk again." He shrugged contemptuously. "Doc ain't never been one to keep his mouth shut!" He stepped towards the seated figure. He held out his hand. "Let's shake on it. I've made you a fair offer. Get yourself back East, man. Hire yourself a nurse . . . "

He never finished his sentence for a

scream of undiluted rage burst from Magnalia. Brewes gaped, surprised, the sound was one you'd expect to hear from a female.

Enraged beyond all reason the crippled man now picked up the kerosene lamp and hurled it with all his might at the hated figure of John Brewes.

Brewes side-stepped.

The lamp thudded against the wall hanging behind John Brewes, glass shattering, kerosene running down the tapestry. The smell of the kerosene instantly permeated the room and orange slivers of flame licked at the hanging, slowly taking hold.

Brewes swore. He would have liked to leave Magnalia but he was damned if he could do it. No 'man' would leave a cripple to burn. Brewes, having his good name to think of, started forward growling angrily. "Well, I guess I'll have to haul you out of here." Magnalia's eyes he saw were wild. Brewes misread the situation reckoning that Magnalia was in fact crazed with fear. He stooped, intending to grip Magnalia beneath the arms, haul him up and haul him out.

"Bastard!" There was a wealth of meaning in that one single word. Fat, pudgy hands reached up and fixed themselves around John Brewes' thick neck. If Brewes' neck had been thinner then the rancher would have been done for. Fingers pressed into flesh, the hate which consumed Magnalia giving him that extra strength he needed.

John Brewes reeled backwards, large and powerful enough to take Magnalia with him. The two of them ended up on the rug, sweat pouring from both of them as they fought, one to kill, one to just escape, for Brewes, even whilst he was being strangled, had noted that the flames were spreading. Fast!

Red lights flashed before Brewes' eyes but he was still able to think that Magnalia was a damn fool, a damn fool for not realizing that if they didn't get out now they'd both of them end as roast meat.

Smoke clogged Brewes' nostrils. Desperately his thumbs searched for Magnalia's eye-sockets; he pushed deep seeking to gouge them out.

There was a second shrill scream and then the hands around his face fell away leaving him retching; he rolled away scarcely able to breath, heart thumping wildly. Nor could he see for the room was thick with smoke. Flames crackled. Disorientated Brewes stumbled to his feet knowing he had but one chance. Not the doorway, he could see the glow of flames blocking the doorway. It had to be the window. Fast, before the smoke overcame him. Pointing himself in the direction he believed the window to be Brewes lurched forward, Magnalia forgotten.

As John Brewes crashed through the glass to land on Magnalia's veranda a bell started to pound. Brewes crawled towards the sound. The house behind him would soon be burning like a furnace. His back pained him. It was burnt he guessed. From the house came one shrill scream and then the crashing sound of wood stoving in, a beam most likely; after that there were no further screams.

Dimly he could hear the cook shouting and cursing, urging the drunken bums to rouse themselves to do something. Brewes could see them now staggering out of the bunkhouse, some of them without their boots.

Wheezing now Brewes forced himself to stand, not wanting the drunken no-goods to see him brought low. Who would have thought it that damn fool Magnalia had gone and killed himself. Unintentionally. If he hadn't been befuddled with whiskey he would not have done it; no man would choose that way to go. Hell, he'd always known that Magnalia was no true rancher. Magnalia was yellow, a fool, and an opportunist. Worst day's work it ever was for Magnalia when he'd chosen to head for Capra. He'd got more than he'd ever bargained for.

Who the hell had dry-gulched

Magnalia? Brewes wished he knew. He'd shake that man by the hand and buy him as much whiskey or brandy as he could drink. That man had done the whole town a damn favour.

* * *

Doggedly Clay worked his way through the saloons, he was tired and irritable and the thought of Gracie working in one of these places caused a slow anger to burn.

The anger subsided when he discovered that Gracie although being hired had not gotten round to work. His lips twitched with amusement as he heard about the incident at the Birdcage but the amusement quickly faded when he heard the outcome of that impetuous act.

The law he decided was a jackass. Clay determined to have words with Gracie forthwith and if that damn fool of a lawman thought he could keep him out then the man would have to think again pretty damn quick. But the lawman, a short, rotund individual was, to Clay's surprise, happy to oblige.

And Gracie wasn't quite the woman he remembered her to be. It hit him then that she was scared. And she hadn't thought he would trouble coming after her.

"What the hell are you doing here, Clay Purnell!" she exclaimed upon catching sight of him but her attempt at bravado failed, her voice shook and her eyes, he was quick to note, were red-rimmed.

He regarded her through the bars of her cell. The cell stank. This wasn't how he had envisaged it would be.

His lips twisted into a dry smile. "I'm here to propose," he rejoined, "and I'd be obliged if you'd say yes."

"Yes. But how, Clay?" She shook her head. "I'll not see you end up on the wanted list for breaking me out of jail. Never. I won't see you hunted down like a dog. I won't . . . "

"Quit talking, Gracie." He was relieved to see she sounded more like her old self. "I've already figured a way to get you out of here. We're getting married first chance and then we're shipping out." He shrugged. "Capra finally rid itself of me. I've been transferred out. First thing I did when I hit this two-bit town was to check over at the telegraph office. Gaskill has wired the details. Seems missionaries are needed overseas, Gracie. London, England."

"You, Clay? What damn foolishness is this!" she exclaimed in disbelief.

"Mrs Brewes. She's behind it. Given the circumstances I ain't sure whether to cuss her or thank her. Leastways we've a place to head for. I guess neither of us wants to see Capra again."

"The further the better I'd say. What's your plan or ain't I permitted to know?"

Concisely he related his plan such as it was.

"It's leaving one or two things

to chance ain't it?" she observed doubtfully.

Clay shrugged. "Best I could come up with. If it don't work I guess I'll have to resort to violence. But one way or another I'll get you out. Be ready Sunday."

As Clay re-entered the outer office the lawman regarded him speculatively. "I didn't hear no screeching or cussing," he observed. "I guess she was glad to see you huh!" He rubbed his chin. "This one now, I ain't worried about anyone getting her out. With the men, I have to tote the keys around with me night and day but with this one I can go fishing or attend church and know she'll still be there when I get back. Damn shame she weren't able to bring the bottle down with sufficient force to finish off that polecat." He paused. "That way I'd not have been obliged to do anything about it. But with him crying murder and my contract coming up for renewal . . . " He shrugged. "Don't pay no heed to my ramblings,

Preacher. I won't delay you. I guess you've got things to attend to."

"I reckon," Clay agreed. He reckoned he and the lawman understood each other perfectly. The lawman was hoping someone would set Gracie free. Clay smiled. He aimed to oblige.

12

CURIOUS to see the inside of the notorious Birdcage saloon Clay found it and went in. Amazed, he stared up at the enormous gilt cages hanging from the ceiling. They were empty now it being early in the day.

"Would you believe it, Minister, come night-time the men are queuing up to get in them there cages," a hard-faced woman observed. "What have you got to say about that?" she winked.

"Not a damn thing," Clay rejoined. Making his way to the bar he ordered a beer. Outside of town a herd was camped. He guessed the drovers would be in as soon as the beef had been loaded into the next freight train out. Drovers were an unpredictable bunch, ill-tempered, stubborn, boisterous and sometimes plain foolish. His face broke into a smile at the thought of the trail boss, Davey Walsh, being hoisted up in one of those contraptions. Davey was fool enough to do it. Years back Clay had hoisted Davey out of the path of stampeding longhorns. Clay drank his beer. It was time now to call in the debt. Drovers were also proud men, men very particular at paying what they owed.

Downing his beer Clay aware of how curiously the scattering of scantily dressed women were observing him headed towards the batwings. As he stepped forward the batwings swung violently inwards, the girl who'd shoved them cannoning into Clay. His hands reached out to steady her.

From the expression on her face he reckoned trouble of one kind or another was coming. Every instinct told him not to involve himself. His feet wanted to walk on away from the damn Birdcage Saloon but his conscience kept him firmly planted.

"What the hell is going on?" The boss and owner of the Birdcage had appeared from a back room, a small, bald-headed, mean-eyed man. Clay's practised eye told him the man wore a shoulder holster beneath his pin-striped suit. Clay thinned his lips. It was provident the little weasel hadn't reached for that gun and shot Gracie. He guessed she'd rendered the weasel semi-conscious. The little louse looked the kind to shoot a woman and right now he was regarding his employee with anger.

Voice shaking for she'd obviously run the length of Main Street the words tumbled out. Some of the women smirked, one hooted with laughter but for the most they looked worried.

"Well!" an older woman declared knowingly, "that no-account lawman won't lift a finger to help you. His contract coming up for renewal and all. You little fool. You've riled them up plenty and now you'll have to face the consequences of it."

"You girls step out of line and you're on your own."

"Please Mr Mills." She regarded her employer in terror. "You've got to help me."

"Ain't no got to about it girl," he rejoined. "Now get the hell out of my saloon. I'll not have you leading them in here. I'll not see my place wrecked." He stepped forward. "Get! Or must I throw you out."

"You damn polecat!" Clay's temper which he had believed to be strictly controlled flared up. This man was the one responsible for Gracie's plight; all along, although he'd not cared to admit it, Clay had been itching to lash out at this man. And he'd now been given the chance. His clenched fist connected with the man's stomach and his other fist struck the polecat soundly on the chin.

"Hell, Preacher, you've knocked him cold." One of the women knelt beside the fallen man. "But he ain't dead!"

"More's the pity," another claimed.

"Why'd you do it?"

They stood around him now regarding him with open curiosity. It had occurred to none of them that he might have felt sorry for the terrified girl the man had been about to boot out on to Main Street. But that wasn't the real reason. He'd done it because of Gracie.

He shrugged. "Let's just say I don't take kindly to the birdcages," he rejoined, seeing immediately that his answer had satisfied them. That they could understand.

He regarded the girl. "I'll handle what's coming." He smiled slightly. "Guess I can't stand idle and watch folk make fools of themselves, do something they'll be ashamed to think about later. Leastways, I'd hope they'd be ashamed."

"No chance of that, Preacher."

"Maybe not," Clay agreed. His shoulders shook.

"You're laughing."

"Womenfolk take some beating." His laughter faded. "I ain't standing idle whilst the men of this town concern themselves in a matter which ain't none of their concern."

"They won't listen to you."

"Sure they will," Clay rejoined. "That's how come the Colt .45 got its name. It keeps the peace." He paused. "Effectively I reckon."

"You don't sound like any preacher I've ever met before!" The older woman regarded him suspiciously. "You sure you're a preacher, Minister?"

"Yup," Clay responded with a smile. "And I've heard those words before." He stepped through the batwings ready to confront the trouble that was heading his way. Regrettably, he reflected, it was true that whilst folk would pay heed to a Peacemaker more often than not they'd pay no heed to words. Especially not his words. He was a stranger in town. He was not their minister and they were all of them fired up over an imagined insult.

And the woman must have been right about that lard barrel of a sheriff.

The man was plainly needed and there was no sign of him.

"I'll be damned!" Clay eyed the rider who'd swung down before the Birdcage. "Davey Walsh. I was aiming to ride on out and say howdy."

"The hell you were Clay Purnell," Davey Walsh rejoined, without preamble. "Is it true? I've heard tell they've got birdcages strung from the ceiling. And I've heard tell that a man can . . . "

"You've heard right, Davey," Clay replied. "Fact is I want a word. After I've dealt with a certain matter first."

"What do you think of my moustache?" Davey asked. "Reckon it'll impress the ladies? I heard tell it would." Since Clay had last seen him the trail boss had grown a long curling moustache. "And by trouble you ain't referring to the folk heading this way?" Davey Walsh guffawed with laughter. "What have you done to rile these good folk? You ain't been up in one of those damn birdcages have you?" he joshed good-naturedly.

"Hell, I thought nothing would surprise me!" Clay exclaimed. "You see what I see, Davey? Their minister, he's tagging on along behind them. He's with them!" Clay spat in disgust. He inclined his head. "Best get inside, Davey. You're to have no part in this do you hear? If you're going to help me I'll need you to be in one piece. I'm calling in that debt you owe me," he said, just so that there could be no mistake. This time he wasn't asking he was telling.

"That serious huh." Davey's air of amusement faded. "Sure," he replied easily, "you can count on me."

"Then get on in the Birdcage," Clay ordered. "I don't want you taking a stray slug." To his relief Davey Walsh, albeit with great reluctance, complied.

Calm now, confident that he had right on his side, Clay stepped out on to Main Street to confront the mob. Farmers most of them he saw. The woman the girl had pushed over in retaliation had been a farming woman.

Two women pushing each other. The farmer's wife first shoving the painted woman off the sidewalk, screeching out that her kind weren't fit to be on the sidewalk with decent women, and then the saloon girl running after the farmer's fat wife and shoving her over.

Unfortunately she'd gone down in a pile of fresh horse-droppings. Hence the fury of the decent folk of the town. And there were womenfolk and children tagging along to see the fun, if taking a lash to a female could be called fun.

Some folk, Clay reflected, had no sense of humour. Just thinking about what had gone on between the two women made him want to laugh. But it was no laughing matter. Violence was a real possibility. And maybe death, although he hoped not. But he would not be swayed. He was damned if he'd allow them to trample over him. That was the only way they'd get at the girl inside the saloon. From inside the saloon came a roar of laughter. He guessed Davey Walsh had heard the sorry tale.

Inside the Birdcage Davey Walsh hauled out his Peacemaker. "I don't reckon they'll get past Clay. He always used to be a mean one, leastways sometimes." Davey grinned. "But if they do I'll blast a few of them myself. Least I can do in Clay's memory."

"His memory!" The girl who'd done the pushing stared wildly at the waddy.

Davey winked. "Yep. Only way they'll get past Clay is to kill him; he's an obstinate . . . er, man," Davey corrected hurriedly as there were females present.

* * *

"That's far enough. This foolishness ends here."

"Ain't you heard what that floozie has done?" a female's voice shouted.

"Yup. As I see it two women have had a falling out. Ain't no call for the rest of you to get involved. I ain't partial to mob rule. Things get out of hand. Folk do things that later make them ashamed." He studied the sea of faces before him. Not that many of them appeared outraged. A good many looked amused, even malicious. He guessed the womenfolk had been stirring things up. "Vengeance ain't yours to take. Leave it to a higher authority," he advised. "The Lord generally manages to deal with wrong-doers in His own good time." Even as he spoke his eyes scanned the crowd seeking the ring leaders. He knew the platitudes he'd come out with had not been enough. Words, leastway from him, would not deflect them from their purpose. He played his last card. "Don't you agree, Minister?" he addressed the town's own preacher.

"I do not," the man replied pompously. "If I had any say in the matter I'd see every one of those fallen women whipped out of town!" At his words a cheer went up.

Upon hearing the words of hate a

man stepped out of the crowd. The self-appointed spokesman. The leader. Leastways at this moment. Clay's eyes narrowed, they rested upon the tightly stretched, purple satin waistcoat, then rose to rest speculatively on the round, red, perspiring face. This man was confident. Confident that one man would not be so foolish to stand alone against many.

"Who are you?" Clay asked.

"I'm the mayor." The other regarded Clay as though that word mayor said it all. No other introduction was necessary. The mayor spread his hands expansively, "As you can see we're not a lynching party. Just decent folk determined to see justice done. That painted woman will merely be given a good thrashing and escorted to the rail depot. A free ticket will be provided and she'll be advised to leave."

"And who aims to administer this thrashing? You?"

"Certainly not," the mayor responded,

outraged at the suggestion. "One of the ladies will administer the thrashing." He paused. "We're decent men as I've told you. Now step aside, Minister. This is not your town. None of this is your concern."

"Yes it is," Clay rejoined. "I know my duty and I aim to do it. Not one of you is going to lay a hand on that girl." He shrugged. "I wouldn't advise any of you to try and walk over me. I'd regard such a move as downright unfriendly."

The mayor's smile did not falter. "Your concern does you credit but . . . "

"Quit gabbing." A big farmer lost patience. "He's bluffing."

Hell no, Clay thought. "Don't . . . " he began, but it was too late, the fool of a farmer reached for his .44 Smith and Wesson. The man was out-classed and if he'd thought at all about the matter he would have known it. Having no choice Clay hauled iron and put a shot into the farmer's leg aiming for the fleshy part.

For good measure he also shot the mayor through the shoulder.

He had no choice. They had to be stopped and stopped now. If Clay were to go down himself before these people the enraged farming men would be quite capable of stomping him to death beneath their Granger boots. He was under no illusions about that.

Womenfolk fled screaming, making themselves scarce now real trouble had started. The minister he saw was fleeing with the women.

To Clay's disbelief as the street cleared the sheriff chose that moment to appear.

"What in tarnation is going on here?" the sheriff asked, as if he had no inkling about anything.

"Fact is," Clay stated coldly, "this man" — he pointed at the farmer — "drew on me. I had to shoot in self-defence." His lips twisted. "The mayor, I'm sorry to say, got hit by a slug that went astray. These things happen when a man stands in close proximity to a Peacemaker."

"You two! Get the mayor to the doc. And the farmer likewise. Least they ain't dead! And the rest of you men get out of here. I reckon you ought to be ashamed of yourself going on the rampage when womenfolk and children were abroad. No telling what could have happened. I'll not have vigilantes in my town."

Face impassive, Clay watched as they slunk away like so many curs. The sheriff mopped his brow. "It's that damn preacher who is behind this. I reckon he stirred things up. That man is a thorn in my side. Well, that was a close thing, son. You'd best make yourself scarce I reckon. Things will simmer down. Next time they'll maybe think before taking the law into their own hands." He wiped his brow. "Sure is hot ain't it? I blame this little fracas on the weather. Makes folk kind of crazy so I've observed. Womenfolk especially."

As Clay walked into the Birdcage

much to his embarrassment the girls started clapping.

"Anything you want it's on the house," one of them said. She winked. "Anything you want. Understand what I mean?"

"I sure do," Clay replied. "But I'll not take up your kind offer. Maybe you'd care to extend it to my pard here. Where's your boss?"

The woman shrugged dismissively. "We won't be seeing him this evening. He's been toted over to Doc's place. Being kept there for observation." She grinned. "Sure enough we'll extend that offer to your pard."

"Hold on there, Davey." Clay caught hold of Davey Walsh's arm. "We'd best have a quiet word. I need to tell you what I want you to do."

Davey Walsh listened in silence. When Clay had finished speaking the trail boss threw back his head and laughed. "You damn fool. I'd advise you against getting hitched but I reckon you're as stubborn as a mule."

"I reckon," Clay agreed.

"Well in that case I'd be happy to oblige, although I reckon I'm doing you a disservice not a favour." A thoughtful expression crossed his face. He winked. "I might even contrive to wreck the Birdcage. It's the least that polecat deserves."

"Do that," Clay agreed with a grin.

* * *

Lying on the hard, narrow bunk Gracie watched a fly as it struggled futilely to escape from a spider's web. Her sympathies lay with the fly. She felt kind of like a fly herself. Their situations were not dissimilar and she knew just how that fly was feeling. Clay had said he would get her out and get her away safely but she could not help fearing that her chance of happiness could yet be snatched away.

And her head felt hot. Damp hot. She reckoned she was coming down with a fever.

* * *

When the cattle came they filled all of Main Street, raising up a cloud of choking dust. Clay followed on behind, riding drag, breathing in the dust despite the bandanna which covered his mouth and nostrils. It would be a fair while before Davey Walsh got his critters out of town, a fair while before the sheriff got out of the church and even longer before the sheriff troubled checking on the condition of the prisoner. They'd be long gone, their tracks obscured.

Clay grinned cheerfully. True to his word Davey Walsh had diverted a few critters skilfully herding them through the batwings of the Birdcage saloon.

13

LIFE, John Brewes reflected, could not be better. Things were more or less going his way. Magnalia was gone and Brewes aimed to buy Magnalia's spread. He'd put the word out that he would not feel kindly disposed if anyone else showed an interest.

Clay Purnell was gone. Gaskill remained but Gaskill could be taken care of. Word was that Isaac Flick and Johnny Chequer were in the territory. Either one of them, Brewes reckoned, stood a good chance of getting Gaskill. They'd come expensive but Brewes was prepared to pay. When he was able to locate either one of them. Like foxes the two top guns seemed to have gone to earth their whereabouts at present unknown.

Taking advantage of his wife's absence

he'd succumbed to temptation and availed himself of what the girls at the Red Garter had to offer. And wished he'd done it sooner. For the girls offered a darn sight more than Mrs Brewes. He'd been thinking a good deal about his wife. Now if the wheel were to come off her buggy for instance, well, he guessed he wouldn't exactly grieve.

Turning over various possibilities he looked down from a room in the Red Garter. "You keep your mouth shut about this. Do you hear?" He didn't turn his head to look at the half-naked female on the bed.

"Sure, honey," she replied, unconcerned by his drastic change of manner, the implied threat in his tone. "Mrs Brewes won't hear about this from any of us girls." She laughed. "Leastways the new preacher won't be no gunman. Ain't nothing for you to trouble yourself over now."

"What the hell do you mean!" Angrily he rounded on the woman, she'd sounded as though she were implying he'd been afraid to lock horns with Clay Purnell. That had never been so.

"Nothing, honey." Her tone was placatory. His complexion had darkened. And she knew an irascible man when she saw one.

"Don't ever call me honey. As far as you and the rest of those no-account whores are concerned my name is Mr Brewes."

She lowered her eyelashes concealing her anger. "Well, Mr Brewes," she drawled, "whole town knows how Clay Purnell made you look a fool." She shrugged. "Although why that man took it into his head to save those two wideloopers I surely can't tell. That's Clay for you. I sure hope he finds Gracie and marries her."

Her words had achieved their objective. She'd aimed to prick Brewes' thick hide. The door closed behind him with a resounding crash. Pride, that was his weakness. He had too much of it. And the thought of folk sniggering, well, he'd not be able to put it out of his head so easily. Mr Brewes indeed!

* * *

Clay had put Capra out of his mind. All he cared about was Gracie and getting her safe on board that ocean-going vessel. He would not rest easy until they were under sail. He was edgy. Something he'd never been before. And he had good reason. The polecat who owned the Birdcage had put up a reward for her capture. Clay hadn't reckoned on the man's vindictiveness. Just as well for he would have been sorely tempted to use his Peacemaker. And he would have done if it had meant Gracie's safety.

Things had not gone as he'd planned. First off Gracie had taken sick, real sick. Needing a place to hole up he'd found himself of necessity back at the stage depot holed up under the same roof as Isaac Flick.

Gracie had damn near died but she'd pulled through and soon they'd be heading out. And about time. He had no wish to continue his acquaintance with Isaac, the man sitting at the table now swilling black coffee and regarding him with a mocking expression.

"You ain't like no minister I've ever met," Isaac Flick observed.

Clay found himself wondering why Flick hadn't ridden on. He'd considered the idea that maybe Flick was attracted to the short-tempered female who ran the depot.

"You're a law-breaker, Minister," Flick continued. "And don't put too much salt in the chicken soup. Can't say I blame your intended for spitting it out. She sure does know how to cuss!" He actually grinned.

"I reckon," Clay agreed, sorely tempted to cuss himself.

"And don't you be forgetting Isaac Flick pays his debts. I owe you."

"Flick, I'm heading somewhere our paths won't ever cross again." He paused. “There’s blood on your hands, Isaac Flick. If it don’t trouble you none it sure as hell ought to.”

“Nope. It don’t trouble me none.” Flick smirked. “I’d say your hands are none too clean, Minister.”

“I ain’t never regretted a Goddamn thing I’ve done,” Clay rejoined.

“Clay Purnell, kindly moderate your language.” Gracie stood in the doorway. “In readiness for your new posting. We’re heading out, Isaac, on the eastbound stage. Guess we won’t be seeing you again. Take care now, do you hear!”

Clay opened and shut his mouth. Gracie seemed kindly disposed towards Isaac Flick. She’d actually observed that he was not as bad as some, leaving Clay to make what he would of that remark. He sniffed. “What’s that smell?” Gracie was dressed in black mourning clothes, complete with black hat and veil. Kindly provided by Josephine. Apparently the garb had been stowed away in readiness.

"Preservative. Keeps the moths out," Gracie replied. "And don't you be too long in the out-house, Isaac. I need . . . "

"Gracie!" Clay exclaimed surprised to observe Isaac Flicks ears turn bright red.

"What?"

"You take some beating." He pulled her into his arms and proceeded to kiss her soundly forgetful of everything else.

* * *

John Brewes approached the depot on foot leading his limping horse, the critter must have turned its foot in a chiseller-hole. His expression was sour. His wife was due in. Soon. And he'd been telegraphed to meet the stage with the buggy. The buggy, well, the woman kept one he could hire. He'd escort Mrs Brewes home but he was damned if he'd drive a buggy.

The sight of Clay Purnell with Gracie

froze him in the doorway. Gracie! Her face was up on the wanted poster. The reward was generous. As he stood there the thought occurred to him that he'd like to see Clay Purnell sweat. Behind bars. Eaten up because Gracie was locked away in an asylum. Hell on earth as far as Clay Purnell were concerned.

Brewes waged war with himself. Part of him said to let them both be. The worst part of him said why he'd surely been given a chance to even the score and he'd be a darn fool not to take it. Stealthily he drew his Peacemaker, the thought occurring to him that Purnell would not be co-operative. In that event he'd have no choice but to blast Clay Purnell.

"Freeze," he ordered. "If either one of you twitch I'll blast you!" They both complied. "Now raise your hands and turn round slowly."

"What the hell is going on, John Brewes?" Gracie demanded, without preamble.

"You really don't know!" Brewes savoured his moment of trouble.

"Nope." She was, he saw, greatly puzzled. She really hadn't guessed.

"Why, Miss Gracie, you're a wanted felon. As a law-abiding citizen I've no choice but to take you in."

"The hell you are Brewes!" Clay had not expected this of Brewes.

John Brewes' mouth curved into a sneer. "You're good, Purnell. I'll concede you that. But you ain't good enough to haul out your Peacemaker before I squeeze the trigger." His eyes narrowed. "You made a fool of me."

"That was not my intention."

"Nope I don't reckon it was," Brewes agreed, "but I'm still taking her in. Think about it, Clay. Gracie locked away for the rest of her days."

Clay took a steadying breath. "You can't do it, Brewes. True we've locked horns but it's over."

"No, it ain't." Brewes knew Purnell would reach for his Peacemaker. A desperate man, Purnell would be prepared to die but it would be his hope to take his enemy with him thus saving Gracie. Brewes waited, prepared to let Purnell hope.

Sweat beaded Clay's brow. Behind John Brewes, approaching stealthily, came Isaac Flick, gun in hand.

"Put the gun down, Brewes. Let us be. Please!"

"You're begging!" John Brewes spat. "Never thought I'd see the day come when Clay Purnell was prepared to beg. Well, let me tell you, even if you were to go down and lick my boots I'd still take her in."

Clay clamped his mouth shut. Part of his mind told him that it was not Isaac Flick's way to pistol whip. Flick's way was to kill.

The sound of the gun broke the silence. John Brewes fell forward to land with a thud upon the floor.

The two coaches rolled in simultaneously. A widow, muffled in black, got aboard the east-bound coach. Clay, who'd been forced to hide out joined the widow at the last moment.

Mrs Brewes raised hell. "I knew he'd not trouble himself," she screeched at her sulking daughter.

After the two stage coaches rolled out Josephine raised hell with Isaac Flick.

"Bury him deep," she ordered. "Along with the other two. If word gets out folk are being blasted at my depot, why, they'd say a female ought never to be in charge in the first place."

"Yes ma'am." Isaac Flick grinned. Clay Purnell and Gracie had that coach to themselves. Isaac reckoned he knew what they might be doing.

"And what are you grinning about?" she snapped.

Isaac Flick picked up the shovel. "Not a thing, ma'am, not a thing." Still smiling he got to digging.

Other titles in the Linford Western Library:

TOP HAND
Wade Everett

The Broken T was big. But no ranch is big enough to let a man hide from himself.

GUN WOLVES OF LOBO BASIN
Lee Floren

The Feud was a blood debt. When Smoke Talbot found the outlaws who gunned down his folks he aimed to nail their hide to the barn door.

SHOTGUN SHARKEY
Marshall Grover

The westbound coach carrying the indomitable Larry and Stretch headed for a shooting showdown.

FIGHTING RAMROD
Charles N. Heckelmann

Most men would have cut their losses, but Frazer counted the bullets in his guns and said he'd soak the range in blood before he'd give up another inch of what was his.

LONE GUN
Eric Allen

Smoke Blackbird had been away too long. The Lequires had seized the Blackbird farm, forcing the Indians and settlers off, and no one seemed willing to fight! He had to fight alone.

THE THIRD RIDER
Barry Cord

Mel Rawlins wasn't going to let anything stand in his way. His father was murdered, his two brothers gone. Now Mel rode for vengeance.

ARIZONA DRIFTERS
W. C. Tuttle

When drifting Dutton and Lonnie Steelman decide to become partners they find that they have a common enemy in the formidable Thurston brothers.

TOMBSTONE
Matt Braun

Wells Fargo paid Luke Starbuck to outgun the silver-thieving stagecoach gang at Tombstone. Before long Luke can see the only thing bearing fruit in this eldorado will be the gallows tree.

HIGH BORDER RIDERS
Lee Floren

Buckshot McKee and Tortilla Joe cut the trail of a border tough who was running Mexican beef into Texas. They stopped the smuggler in his tracks.

BRETT RANDALL, GAMBLER
E. B. Mann

Larry Day had the choice of running away from the law or of assuming a dead man's place. No matter what he decided he was bound to end up dead.

THE GUNSHARP
William R. Cox

The Eggerleys weren't very smart. They trained their sights on Will Carney and Arizona's biggest blood bath began.

THE DEPUTY OF SAN RIANO
Lawrence A. Keating and Al. P. Nelson

When a man fell dead from his horse, Ed Grant was spotted riding away from the scene. The deputy sheriff rode out after him and came up against everything from gunfire to dynamite.

FARGO: MASSACRE RIVER
John Benteen

The ambushers up ahead had now blocked the road. Fargo's convoy was a jumble, a perfect target for the insurgents' weapons!

SUNDANCE: DEATH IN THE LAVA
John Benteen

The Modoc's captured the wagon train and its cargo of gold. But now the halfbreed they called Sundance was going after it . . .

HARSH RECKONING
Phil Ketchum

Five years of keeping himself alive in a brutal prison had made Brand tough and careless about who he gunned down . . .